S0-AIB-820

$4.99 US / $6.99 CAN.

ISBN 0-446-61683-4

9 780446 616836

5 0 4 9 9

EAN

SANDRA BROWN

DBU237297

LOVE BEYOND REASON

Chapter One

✧ ✧

The Denver City Council voted today to increase taxes by six percent for the coming fiscal year. Councilmen argued that—"

"Great," grumbled Katherine, "that's just what I need—another drain on the budget." She replaced the hairbrush she had been using in the well-organized drawer and reached for a bottle of lotion on the bathroom dressing table. She rested her leg on the commode seat as she smoothed a liberal application of the emollient to her long, shapely leg. She returned her attention to the voice coming from the radio on her bedside table in the adjoining bedroom.

"An armed man's attempt to rob a convenience store

1

was thwarted today by Denver police. A tactical squad surrounded the building after receiving a call . . .''

Higher taxes and crime. What a wonderful note to end the day on, Katherine thought ruefully as she brushed her teeth.

Was this to be one of those nights when she allowed herself to wallow in self-pity and bitterness? Such introspection was rare, but she indulged herself whenever this melancholy mood settled over her.

It would be nice to say good night to someone, share a room, space, with him, breathe the same air, hear the same sounds. Him? Why had this nonentity taken a masculine form? She sighed. Living alone had its compensations, but it could be lonely too.

"Tomorrow's weather . . .''

Frowning, Katherine glanced at the radio and wondered if the late-night announcer ever got weary of talking to himself. Did he ever think about the souls he was talking to? Did he sense their loneliness and strive with his easy chatter to ease that solitude?

His voice was pleasant. It was well-modulated and distinct, but somewhat . . . sterile. His casual bantering was rehearsed, anonymous, and impersonal.

God! What a dour mood I'm in, she chided herself as she pulled on her robe and left the bathroom. *Maybe I should get a roommate now that Mary is married*, mused Katherine as she went through the house on one last inspection before turning out the lights.

Katherine loved this old house. After her father died when she was barely six years old, her mother had managed to keep the house and had reared Katherine and her younger sister, Mary, as comfortably as she could on her postal clerk's salary. It hadn't been easy for the widow, but forced frugality had taught the girls to live economically.

Katherine checked the door locks and switched off the living-room lights just as she rejected the idea of a roommate. She and Mary had gotten along fine after their mother's death three years before, but they were sisters, and Mary's cheerful disposition made her easy to live with. Katherine might not be so lucky with someone else.

Mary. Dear Mary. Her life certainly hadn't improved with her marriage. *No, thank you*, Katherine thought wryly. She would remain independent and suffer through these short, though painful, spurts of loneliness.

"This bulletin just came in . . ."

Katherine reached for the button on the radio to set her alarm when she recoiled, staring fixedly at the wood-and-chrome box and listening in disbelief to what the announcer was saying.

"Tonight Peter Manning, a prominent figure in Denver's business community, was tragically killed when his car spun out of control and crashed into a concrete abutment. Police reported that Mr. Manning's car left the road at a high rate of speed. He was pronounced dead at the scene. An unidentified woman, riding on the passenger side of the sports car, was also killed in the tragic accident. Peter Manning was the son—''

Katherine jumped when her telephone rang stridently at her side. She took deep gasping breaths before her trembling hand grabbed the receiver. She sank onto the bed as she raised the instrument to her ear. "Yes?" she wheezed.

"Miss Adams?"

"Yes."

"This is Elsie. I work here at the Manning estate. I met you—''

"Yes, Elsie, I remember you. How is my sister?" she asked urgently.

"That's why I'm calling, Miss Adams. Have you heard about Mr. Peter?"

It wasn't necessary to tell the maid that she hadn't been officially notified, but confirmed that she knew of Peter's accident.

"Well, all hell's broken loose over here. Mrs. Manning is hysterical, screaming and yelling. Mr. Manning is little better. Photographers and reporters are all over the place talking and waving cameras and microphones and flashing lights—''

"How is Mary?" Katherine interrupted imperiously.

"I'm coming to that. When the policeman told them about the wreck, they were all in the living room. When he mentioned that a woman was in the car with Peter, and that she was dead too, Mrs. Manning turned to Miss

Mary, who is so sweet, and started yelling at her. She said such awful things to her, Miss Adams. She said if Miss Mary had been a better wife, Mr. Peter wouldn't have gone out at night to look—''

"Please, Elsie, is Mary all right?"

"No, Miss Adams, she isn't. She ran up the stairs to her room to escape Mrs. Manning. No one was paying any attention to her, even in her condition. I went in to check on her and she's bleeding, Miss Adams."

"Oh, God—"

"Yes, and she's in labor, I think. I thought you ought to know 'cause nobody around here seems to care about her. They're all thinking about—"

"Elsie, listen carefully. Call an ambulance. Get Mary to the hospital right away. I'll call her obstetrician. Don't tell anyone what you're doing. If you have to sneak Mary out through the kitchen, do it. Just get her in the ambulance. Okay?"

"Yes, Miss Adams, I will. I always liked your sister and thought—"

"Never mind all that now, Elsie. Just call the ambulance." Katherine couldn't afford to be exasperated by Elsie's garrulity, but she hoped the excited woman would get Mary to the hospital immediately.

Katherine cut that connection and quickly dialed the doctor after fumbling through the telephone book frantically searching for his number. Alphabetical order seemed to have escaped her, and she cursed her ineptitude. She reached his answering service and quickly

5

apprised the operator of her sister's condition. The operator promised to contact the doctor immediately and have him go directly to the hospital.

Without thinking about her actions, Katherine stripped off her robe and nightgown and dashed to her closet. Pulling on a pair of jeans, she damned the Mannings and especially Peter. How could he? Hadn't he made Mary's life miserable enough without humiliating her by getting himself killed while another of his women was in the car with him? She believed Mary's tales of his physical abuse, but would that extend to his inducing her labor to deliver a seven-month fetus? *God, help her,* Katherine prayed while pulling a T-shirt over her head and stepping into a pair of sandals.

Without combing her hair or bothering to apply any makeup, she ran out of the house, climbed into her car, and headed for the designated hospital. She forced herself to drive slower than she felt compelled to do. She would be no help to Mary if she were injured or killed herself.

Mary, Mary, why didn't you see the kind of man Peter Manning was? Had she been so blindly captivated by the smile that graced the society page columns that she couldn't see the superficiality of it? Peter Manning, the Golden Boy, son of one of the wealthiest and most prominent families in Denver, heir apparent to bank directorships, real estate holdings, insurance companies, and numerous other enterprises, had become Mary Adams's husband a year ago.

Katherine had been puzzled to say the least when Peter's attention had suddenly become riveted on Mary, whom he had met while she was working in an art gallery to help pay for art classes.

He was suave, debonair, devastatingly handsome, polished, and confident. He had swept gentle, naive, trusting Mary off her feet and then let her fall. Hard and far.

Why? From the outset of that bizarre romance that question had plagued Katherine. Mary was pretty, but nothing like the dazzling debutantes and celebrities Peter was accustomed to escorting. Why had he bothered with Mary?

Katherine honked belligerently at a motorist who was sitting through a green light. Her anger wasn't directed toward the other driver, however. It was directed toward the man who had turned a laughing, happy, vibrant young woman into a haunted, listless robot.

After only a few months of marriage, Peter's loving attitude toward his wife, which Katherine had always felt was a little too overdone to be sincere, began to change drastically.

Katherine had been shocked to listen as Mary tearfully related one horror story after another. Physical and emotional abuse were daily occurrences. Peter was furious over Mary's pregnancy, though she swore he had raped her one night without giving her time to take precautions against that condition. The marriage was a living nightmare.

7

But the picture Peter presented to the world was one of marital bliss. With total devotion he doted on Mary in front of his parents and their country club friends. His hypocrisy would have been laughable if it weren't so tragic.

Katherine wheeled into the hospital's emergency entrance and thankfully found a parking space near the door. She locked her car and raced for the well-lighted alcove only moments before she heard the wail of the ambulance.

She and Mary's doctor were standing in the wide foyer as the paramedics guided the stretcher through the glass doors which opened automatically. Katherine gasped when she saw her sister's face. She covered her mouth to stifle a scream. Mary's eyes were open, but unfocused, and didn't register her sister's presence as they whisked her past Katherine and into one of the treatment rooms.

After a cursory examination Mary was sent to the maternity ward where she delivered a baby girl after only thirty minutes of labor.

The doctor looked bleak as he walked toward Katherine down the hushed, softly lit corridor in his rubber-soled shoes.

"She's in a bad way, Miss Adams. I don't think she'll last the night." Katherine slumped against the wall and stared at him over the tight fist she was pressing hard against her bruised lips. Her green eyes overflowed with tears that flooded over the lower lids, coursing down her pale apricot cheeks. They dampened the strands of honey-gold hair that tumbled around her head in heedless disarray.

"I'm sorry to be so blunt, but I think you ought to know the severity of her condition. She hemorrhaged so much before she got here that there was little we could do about it, though I transfused her." The doctor paused and studied Katherine before saying softly, "It hasn't been a happy pregnancy. She wouldn't take care of herself. I've been worried about her before. . . . Well, I know what happened tonight. I'm sorry about Mr. Manning. I don't think Mary wants to live," he added sympathetically.

Katherine nodded mutely. As the doctor was turning away, she grabbed his sleeve and asked hoarsely, "The baby?"

He gave her a ghost of a smile. "A little girl. Four pounds. Perfectly formed. She should make it."

❧❧ ❧❧

Mary died at dawn. In one of her few lucid moments during the long night, she asked for Katherine.

"A piece of paper," she whispered.

"Paper?" Katherine repeated stupidly. Didn't Mary realize this was their farewell?

"Yes, please, Katherine. Hurry." She could barely form the words.

Katherine searched the hospital room desperately

looking for a piece of paper, and finally found a paper towel in the small bathroom.

"Pen." Mary croaked.

Katherine supplied that out of her purse and watched in wonder as her weakened sister managed to write several lines on the towel with a shaking hand. She signed her usual signature at the bottom when she was finished.

Mary fell against the pillows, totally exhausted. The exertion left her face white and beaded with perspiration. Her lips were blue. Dark circles ringed her eyes, but they were brighter, more alive and vivid than they had been since her marriage. Katherine caught a shadowy glimpse of the former Mary in this wasted shell and wanted to weep copiously for her loss.

Mary was blond and blue-eyed. Her skin had always been clear and rosy. Her eyes had laughed whenever her cherub mouth had curled into the slightest suggestion of a smile. She was shorter and plumper than her svelte sister and agonized over every calorie, until recently when all appetite vanished. The cheerful voice that was now subdued to a gasping whisper brought Katherine back from her reveries.

"Katherine, name her Allison. Don't let them have her. They mustn't have her." The white, clawlike hands gripped Katherine's forearm. "Take her away from here. Tell her I loved her very much." She closed her eyes and breathed a few shallow breaths. When her eyes opened again, they had taken on a dreamlike quality.

They were peaceful. "Allison's such a pretty name. Don't you think so, Katherine?"

※ ※

The double funeral took place two days later. It was a circus. The public's voracious appetite for scandal was fed by the eager reporters competitively trying to write the most sensational story. The girl who had been killed with Peter was a seventeen-year-old high-school cheerleader. Her body had been only partially clothed when the accident occurred. Allison's premature birth and Mary's subsequent death only added more spice to the tantalizing story.

Katherine was saturated with grief over Mary's death. Peter had died instantly from a broken neck without a mark on him. Sadistically, Katherine thought that to be unjust, especially when she remembered Mary's ravaged face, her innocent beauty marred by months of physical abuse and verbal attacks. It wasn't fair.

Katherine had barely been able to cope with the ostentation of the society wedding a year earlier, but the funeral was even more of an ordeal.

Eleanor Manning, managing to look lovely in her black designer dress and well-coiffed blond hair, was inconsolable. One minute she was clinging to Peter Manning, Sr., who was a tall, distinguished, gray-haired man, weeping uncontrollably. The next moment she berated poor dead Mary for not loving Peter, her darling son, enough. Then she would curse Jason, Peter's younger brother, for not being in attendance.

"It wasn't enough that he humiliated us by not attending the wedding. He had to further our shame by not coming home for his brother's funeral. Africa! My God, he's as barbaric as those heathens who live there. First it was Indians. Now it's pagans in Africa!" At that point she would lapse into another bout of hysterical tears.

Katherine knew very little about the brother, Jason Manning. Peter had always referred to him vaguely, as if his existence was of no consequence. Mary, however, had been excited when she received a letter from him.

During a visit with Katherine she exhibited the letter with timid pride. It had never taken much to make Mary happy.

"I got a letter from Peter's brother, Katherine. He's in Africa, you know. He works with oil or something. Anyway, he apologized about not being able to get away for the wedding and congratulated me on the baby. Listen." She read from the plain white stationery which was slashed with a bold, black scrawl.

" 'I look forward to returning home and greeting you as a proper brother should. If you're as pretty as the pictures Mother sent me, I wish I had seen you first. Damn Peter. He's got all the luck!' Of course, he's only teasing me," said Mary blushing. "Doesn't he sound nice? He says, 'Take care of that new niece or nephew of mine. It'll be great to have a baby around, won't it? Just think. I'll be Uncle Jace.' "

Katherine nodded enthusiastically, though it was really out of politeness. She was alarmed by how thin Mary was growing despite her expanding abdomen. On that particular day, she had been much more interested in her sister's declining health and obvious unhappiness than in a long-lost brother. She shelved her impressions of him along with those she had formed about the other Mannings.

After the funeral the days fell into a dull, grinding, and exhausting routine. Katherine went to work every day at the electric company and continued writing the research papers and press releases that she had been hired to do five years ago. Was it really that long since she had graduated from college? Had she been doing this same tedious job that long? She made a respectable salary, but she saw the job only as practice for better things to come. She was a more gifted writer than her job demanded and she longed to have her creativity challenged. Maybe with the new responsibility of a baby, she would be compelled to go looking for a higher-paying job.

Allison! Katherine delighted in her. Every night she visited the hospital and gazed at her niece through the glass wall of the premature-baby nursery. She longed for the day she could hold her. Allison was gaining weight every day, and the pediatrician told the anxious aunt when the baby maintained five pounds for five days he would release her into Katherine's care.

She made arrangements to take two weeks' vacation at the time she could bring Allison home and started scouting out the best day-care center for working mothers. It would have to be the best before she would entrust Allison into its care. It never occurred to her that her guardianship of the baby would be jeopardized.

She was bolted out of her placidity when the Mannings' lawyer called upon her at work. Inundating her desk with official-looking papers, he told her in his prissy, arrogant voice that his clients ". . . intend to take sole responsibility for the child."

"My clients are prepared to take the child and rear her as their own. Of course, for your time, trouble, and expense these past few weeks that she's been in the hospital, you will be compensated."

"You mean bought off, don't you?"

"Please, Miss Adams, I think you are misinterpreting the purpose of my clients. They are financially able to rear the child in an opulent environment. Surely you want what's in the best interest of the child?"

"The mother felt it in her child's best interest that I rear her." Wisely she refrained from telling him of the handwritten instructions.

"I'm sure the father's wishes would have differed greatly." Katherine hated his condescending attitude. "Besides, this discussion is academic. I'm sure no court would award guardianship of a child to a single working-girl with indeterminate morals, when such an illustrious couple as the Mannings are more than willing to take responsibility for their only grandchild, the heir and offspring of their eldest son.''

The insult to her character was so unethical that Katherine didn't honor it with a comment, but she knew that he was threatening her. She could well imagine him saying words to that effect in a courtroom, and it chilled her to the bone to predict what the outcome of such a custody hearing would be.

Katherine stifled her initial panic and tried to reason through her predicament. Uppermost in her mind was the determination that Allison would not grow up under Eleanor Manning's tutelage. She didn't underestimate the Mannings' influence and power. They must have many friends in high places. She and Allison had to get away from them. Plans were made and she carried them out with dispatch.

The pediatrician agreed to release Allison from the hospital a few days earlier than he had originally planned with the condition that Katherine bring the infant to his office the following week. Katherine hated lying, but solemnly promised she would have the baby there.

She called a realtor and discussed the sale of her house. Whatever monies were made were to be put into a savings account in Allison's name. That could be collected later along with any interest accrued. All the furnishings in the house were to be sold, except what Katherine would take with her. The realtor could keep that money in payment for her trouble.

Katherine rented a safety deposit box and, after making a copy of the pitiful paper-towel document, lovingly folded it into the metal box.

She didn't answer her telephone and covered her movements well. Her car was parked away from the house, and she sacrificed the use of lights after dark. Fearful of being presented with a subpoena, she strove for invisibility.

She packed everything she possibly could in the small compact car. Her emotions were running high as she picked up Allison from the hospital.

Katherine gently lay her in the car bed that was strapped by the safety belt onto the front seat of the car. She leaned over and placed a soft kiss on the velvet forehead.

"I don't know much about being a mother," she whispered to the sleeping child. "But then you don't know a lot about being a baby either."

Gazing down into Allison's sweet face that so reminded her of Mary, she felt at ease for the first time since hearing of Peter's death.

As she left Denver, she allowed herself no poignant backward glances toward the mountains or thoughts about selling the house that had been the only home she remembered. She thought of the future, hers and Allison's. From now on, they had no past.

Katherine straightened her back and hunched her shoulders to stretch the cramped muscles. She was sitting on the newspaper-lined living room floor of her garage apartment. For the past half-hour she had been painting a chest of drawers for Allison's room. The evening before she had applied the final coat of glossy blue to the wood surface and was now adding a contrasting yellow stripe. The yellow paint had spotted the newspaper and a few drops had landed on Katherine's bare legs.

Dipping the fine brush into the paint can, she sighed with contentment. Everything had turned out well for her and Allison. Under any circumstances, traveling halfway across the country by oneself with a newborn baby in tow would be an intimidating project. Katherine had left Denver under the grimmest of circumstances, yet the trip had gone smoothly. Allison was an angel of a baby, sleeping every minute that Katherine wasn't changing or feeding her.

Katherine never remembered living in Van Buren, Texas, but her family had lived in the small town before her father's insurance company had offered him a better job in Denver.

Katherine remembered her mother reminiscing about east Texas and its verdant landscape and deep woods. The pictures she painted of it belied the stereotypical depictions of Texas that portrayed vast barren landscapes with tumbleweeds being tossed about by incessant winds. Katherine, after driving through miles of country like that in west Texas, was surprised to find that Van Buren was just as her mother had described it—a peaceful, quaint college town nestled in the piny woods.

Glancing out her wide windows now, Katherine delighted in the sight of the six pecan trees that grew in the yard separating her garage apartment from Happy Cooper's house.

Her new landlady had proved to be a godsend. Katherine had reached Van Buren just as the college's spring term was ending and was lucky enough to secure the apartment which for the past two years had been shared by two Van Buren College coeds. The apartment, having two bedrooms, a living room, kitchen, and bath, was spacious.

Katherine lay her paintbrush aside and walked on silent bare feet into the room she had designated as Allison's, though they both slept in it. Leaning over the repainted crib she had found in a second-hand store, she looked at her niece. The infant's rapid growth was amazing. In the two months they had been in Van Buren, she had gained weight and filled out to become a plump, happy baby despite her inauspicious birth.

Katherine smiled at Allison and scooted a stuffed bunny from under a chubby hand before settling a light blanket over her.

Katherine enjoyed her days off when she could be alone with the baby. She had miraculously secured a job in the public relations office of the college, but was concerned about Allison's care during the day. Much to her surprise, Happy had timidly offered to keep the baby. When Happy made the unexpected suggestion, Katherine had stared at her, smiled, laughed, then to her own amazement and Happy's alarm, began to cry.

What would she have done without Happy, who was a frustrated grandmother who rarely got to see her grand-children? She had two grown daughters who lived with their families on each coast, and a son who lived and worked in Louisiana. He was still single, and Happy mourned his marital status at least once a day. Having been married for forty-three years before being wid-owed, Happy couldn't imagine anyone voluntarily liv-ing alone.

Yes, everything was going well. Katherine's job was surely more interesting than what she had been doing in Denver. Her boss sometimes struck her as odd, for he had the annoying habits of staring, perspiring, and lick-ing his lips. But overlooking his peculiarities, she liked her work.

Scratching her nose absentmindedly, she unknow-ingly smeared yellow paint across it. Then softly hum-ming to herself, she rose from the floor to answer a knock at the door. It wouldn't be Happy. She usually didn't take the time or effort to knock.

Katherine tugged on the bottom of the short, ragged cutoffs she was wearing, hoping that whoever was at the door wouldn't be offended by her appearance.

"Yes?" she said, opening the door.

Had she been about to say anything else, it would have been impossible. The man who filled the doorway was the most spectacular-looking man she had ever seen. If his size weren't enough to distinguish him, certainly the raven black hair and startling blue eyes would have been.

He gave Katherine the same intent inspection she was giving him, and his sensual mouth curved into an amused grin when he took in her disheveled state. Knowing she was going to be working at home all day, she hadn't bothered to do anything more with her honey-colored hair than sweep it up into a careless knot on the top of her head and secure it with pins haphazardly stuck in at varying angles. Tendrils, bleached by the sun, brushed against her cheeks and clung damply to her neck.

Her skin was flushed with color from exertion and the humid warmth of the late summer morning. The extremely short and faded cutoffs were topped by an equally ragged chambray shirt whose sleeves had been cut out long ago either by Katherine or Mary. She had tied the shirttail in a knot under her breasts. It was a good shirt to paint in, but was far from being appropriate attire for greeting guests.

Katherine's first impulse was to slam the door and protect herself from further embarrassment, but the man stared straight into her wide, green eyes and said with no inflection, "I'm Jason Manning."

Chapter Two

❦ ❦

His announcement hit her like a blow in the stomach and robbed her of logical thought. She stood stupefied for several seconds before she slumped against the door frame. She expelled her breath, having held it since opening the door and catching sight of this magnificent man who was Peter Manning's brother.

When she didn't reply or show any inclination toward inviting him in, he said mockingly, "I'm not in the habit of ravishing young women, Miss Adams. And though I've been in Africa for the better part of two years, I'm still civilized."

His eyes were twinkling with mirth, and Katherine

automatically resented his humor. He was going to destroy the world she had so painstakingly built for herself and Allison, and he had the gall to stand there and smile!

"May I come in?" he asked politely, and begrudgingly Katherine moved aside and allowed him to come through the door. She closed it behind him, then changed her mind and opened it again. He caught her move and smiled even deeper. The dimples on either side of his mouth were his only resemblance to Peter. His teeth showed incredibly white in his dark face.

"Still afraid I'm here to do you bodily harm?" he asked teasingly. Then he assumed a serious face and said softly, "Seeing you in that outfit, I'll admit the prospect is damned tempting, but I would never take advantage of a lady with paint on her face."

Katherine glanced down at her atrocious clothes and gasped as she noted how closely the damp cloth was clinging to her breasts. While she was bathing Allison, as was usually the case, she had become drenched. She had forgotten until now that her shirt had been soaked by the time she put the baby down for her nap.

Oh, God! she mentally groaned. She risked looking up at Jason Manning, but he was bending down from his tremendous height to pick up a wet cloth she had used to wipe away the dripping acrylic paint. Fascinated, like one hypnotized, she watched him approach her and reach out to grasp her chin in his fingers.

He tilted her head back so he could see what he was doing as he applied the cloth to the spot of paint on her nose. He went about his job absorbedly, unemotionally, but Katherine was finding it difficult to breathe. His whole presence was overwhelming, suffocating. The fingers on her jaw were strong, but gentle. His skin was very dark. Tans like that weren't acquired by short periods of exposure to the sun while lying coated with thick applications of suntan lotion.

The lines that fanned from the corners of his eyes like fine webs were another indication that he spent most of his time out of doors. Oil? Wasn't that what Mary had said? She couldn't remember. She couldn't remember anything. Her brain had been swept clean when he came toward her and clasped her chin in his hand.

His eyes were surrounded by thick, short, black lashes and framed by raven black brows that arched and tapered as if painted on. Katherine was on eye level with his chest and by raising her eyes only slightly, she could see his strong column of throat. In the deep V of his open sport shirt collar, she saw curling black hair that undoubtedly covered his broad chest. God! What was she thinking?

Angry with herself for allowing him such familiarity, she pushed his hand away and stepped backward.

"What do you want, Mr. Manning?"

He shrugged and dropped the cloth back onto the newspapers spread under his feet. "A Coke would be nice." He smiled beguilingly.

"That isn't what I meant and you know it," she snapped. She was furious in her desperation. His friendly manner was only a ploy to reduce her suspicions and relax her guard. Well, she had resisted the advances of one Manning. Shivering in disgust, she remembered Peter's behavior toward her. I'll resist this Manning too. "What are you doing here?" she inquired coldly.

He sighed and crossed the room to sit on the sofa, the cushions of which she had so proudly recovered herself.

"I think my reason for being here would be obvious to you, Katherine." The sound of her name coming from his mouth made her heart lurch. Were they on a first-name basis already? Another of his disarming tricks, no doubt.

He studied her a moment as he leaned negligently back against the cushions of the couch. "I came to get my brother's baby."

She had known his purpose, but having him verbalize it struck terror in her heart. The pain in her chest was almost more than she could bear. She wasn't going to crumple in front of him. She couldn't!

Her face paled considerably, and, slowly shaking her head, she choked out, "No."

When he saw her distress, he stood and took a few steps toward her. She backed away from him, and when he read the aversion on her face, he stopped. Raking his fingers through hair that would forever be somewhat unruly, he muttered a curse under his breath.

He pulled his bottom lip through his teeth several

times and stared at her through squinted eyes. He stood with his hands on his hips, and the commanding stance made Katherine feel even more vulnerable in her shabby clothes and bare feet. She shifted uncomfortably from one foot to another, but met his stare with as much calm as she could muster.

Finally he spoke. "Look. I know this isn't going to be easy on anyone. So could we at least try to make it as painless as possible? I really would like a Coke if you have one. A cup of coffee? Let's discuss our mutual problem like rational grown-ups. Okay?"

"I have no problem, Mr. Manning."

"Jace."

"What?" she asked, momentarily distracted by his interruption.

"Call me Jace."

"Oh. Well, as I was saying, I have no problem. I love my sister's baby as if she were my own. On her deathbed Mary commissioned me to take care of her, to rear her, to prevent her from ever coming under the influence of any Manning. I have rocked her, bathed her, fed her—"

"*You* fed her?" His eyes went to her breasts, and Katherine flushed hotly in embarrassment and anger. And why were her nipples pressing so tautly against her shirt? Ever since Jace had touched her, she had been self-consciously aware of them being unrestrained under the chambray. A bra had seemed an unnecessary garment when she dressed that morning. This man was threatening in ways other than taking Allison away from her, and she was incapable of dealing with any of them.

Jace was still looking at her with that annoying, amused grin, and she lashed out at him. "Don't be obtuse, Mr. Manning. You know that at the hospital babies are put on a formula if the mother can't or doesn't want to . . . to . . ."

"Breast feed?" he asked softly, intimately.

Katherine looked out the window, then at her bare feet—anywhere to escape those penetrating eyes. She swallowed the lump in her throat before she mumbled, "Yes." She hurried past him on her way to the kitchen. The business of getting him a drink would cover her acute embarrassment. "I'll get you a drink."

She went through the kitchen door practically at a run and braced herself against the counter as if she had reached a haven of repose. Breathing heavily, she put both hands to her pounding temples and asked herself in a critical whisper, "What is the matter with me?"

This person . . . this man—and, God, what a magnificent man!—had totally disconcerted her. She was trembling. There was a tickling sensation in her thighs. She had attributed it to the strings on the legs of her cutoffs, but now admitted it was coming from within. She pressed the palms of her hands flat against her nipples, willing them to return to their relaxed state.

"Can I help?"

Katherine jumped as she heard the voice so close

28

behind her. "W-what? Oh, no. What did you want? A Coke?"

"Yeah, that'd be nice." He hitched a thumb over his shoulder. "What do you call that color on the walls of the living room?"

She was nervously unscrewing the cap on a bottle of Coke she had found in the refrigerator. How long had it been there? What if it was flat? "The color? Oh, it's called terra cotta." She rattled the glass as she set it on the counter and reached for the ice in the freezer. The ice tray stuck and she almost broke a fingernail trying to pry it out.

"It's pretty. How'd you ever think of it? Isn't it a bit unusual?"

She laughed in spite of herself. "You should have seen my landlady's face when I asked permission to paint the room and showed her the sample. She thought I was crazy, but then finally agreed to it. You see, my sister Mary——" she broke off remembering suddenly who he was and why he was here.

He sensed her reticence and gently urged, "Yes? Your sister Mary . . . ?"

Katherine turned away from him and poured the Coke down the side of the ice-filled glass. "Mary was an artist. Sometimes for fun we'd plan rooms and imagine them in outlandish colors. One night she planned a room with orange walls, and surprisingly, we liked it. I've wanted to do a room like that ever since."

She extended the glass of Coke to him and he nodded

his thanks. He moved aside and let her go before him back into the living room.

"Who's going to carry the firewood up the stairs?" he asked completely out of context.

His perception and keen observations were uncanny and disturbing. "Happy, my landlady, asked me the same thing. But I like fireplaces and hated seeing this one going to waste. A former tenant had bricked it in. I had it reopened. I guess I'll have to bring up the firewood one log at a time."

She stepped around the newspapers and the naked-looking chest of drawers. She had pulled out all the drawers for easier painting and stripped them of their hardware. He would think she was terribly messy. But why should his opinion of her matter?

"Please excuse this mess. I needed to do this on my day off, and I have to do it indoors so I'll be close to the baby." She could have bitten her tongue. Why did she make that reference to Allison? Somehow she hoped he would forget his objective and just go away. Did she want him to go away? *Yes!* she averred silently, but was not quite convinced.

He drained the Coke and put the glass on the coffee table after carefully taking a coaster out of its rack. Didn't he ever make a mistake, do anything wrong?

From the basket on the coffee table he picked up an orange spiked with whole cloves and sniffed it appreciatively. Replacing it, he reached for a bright green

Granny Smith apple and gave it the same clinical analysis.

Katherine watched him warily as he crossed the room and stood in front of the large windows looking out over the tree-shaded yard. The white shutters had been pushed aside to allow Katherine a vista of the green expanse she loved.

Palms out, his hands slid into the back pockets of his jeans, and Katherine noticed that he could barely squeeze them between the layers of fabric which stretched so tightly across his slim hips.

The muscles of his shoulders and back stirred the cloth of his plaid cotton shirt. The cuffs had casually been rolled up to just under his elbows. She had never given such avid attention to a man before. But then had she ever seen legs so long and lean and—

"Nice trees," he observed. No comment was required, so she didn't offer one. Long moments of silence passed before he turned to her and asked softly, "Can I see the baby now?"

"She's sleeping," Katherine tried.

He didn't buy it. "I promise not to wake her."

She wanted to refuse him, but it would be useless. If he wanted to see the baby, she couldn't physically stop him. She sighed resignedly and indicated the room where Allison was taking her nap, completely unaware of the friction her existence generated between these two people.

Jace's large body seemed to fill the room as he bent over the crib and pulled back the light blanket.

Allison was in her usual sleeping position. She lay on her stomach, her head turned to one side, her knees drawn up under her tummy, her bottom stuck up in the air.

Katherine carefully watched Jace's reaction as he studied the baby whose gentle, rapid breath was the only sound in the close room. He reached out with one large brown hand and stroked the rosy cheek with his index finger.

"Hello, Allison," he whispered.

Katherine, who had been awed by the contrast of his hand against Allison's small head, turned quickly to look at him. "How did you know her name?" she asked. She had been mindful not to mention it to him, thinking that the less of an individual the baby seemed to him, the less he would want her.

"The nurses at the hospital told me. When I started looking for you, that was the first place I went. They remembered Allison well. The circumstances of her birth and Mary's—" he broke off mid-sentence and looked at Katherine. Was it pain she saw in his eyes? "Anyway, they remembered her. And you."

"Me?"

"Oh, yes, I was told countless times how sweet and considerate you were. Not to mention how beautiful." His voice was a hoarse whisper, and Katherine avoided the blue eyes that looked at her from a face far too close to her own. She could feel his breath fanning her cheek.

Her hands were trembling as she drew the blanket over Allison again. Jace's hand touched her shoulder as if to turn her toward him, but she recoiled and jerked away.

"Don't," she cried. When Allison jumped in reaction to the loud noise, she lowered her voice to a rasping hiss. "How dare you come in my house and act civilly and friendly and . . . and affectionately. Understand me, Mr. Manning. No one is taking Allison away from me. Especially someone named Manning. I want nothing to do with any of you. I ask nothing of you, and neither will Allison." She drew a deep, ragged breath. "Your brother killed my sister!"

The words hung in the room between them. Momentarily they were frozen in time, adversaries assessing each other and weighing the opponent's strength.

The atmosphere crackled with emotion and expectation. Later in private, self-analyzing torment, Katherine swore that she hadn't leaned toward him, that the lunge that brought them together had been solely on his part. All she could truly recall was being enfolded in his powerful warmth. The lips that crushed hers were bruising and hard, and she matched his anger by meeting them in kind. She clutched his back as he wrapped her in arms of steel.

At what point the kiss changed character Katherine

was never able to discern. But for some reason, it was no longer her aim to punish, but to please. She opened her mouth to his demanding tongue and, sensing her acquiescence, his plunder became sweet exploration. They sipped each other as if unable to quench a terrible thirst. Then their mouths fused together again.

"Yoo-hoo, Katherine. There's the strangest-looking car outside. I got worried about you so thought I'd check—"

Happy Cooper's immense proportions filled the doorway to Allison's bedroom and she stood transfixed as she saw Jace standing with Katherine next to the crib.

At the sound of her voice they had sprung apart, stunned by what had happened between them. Katherine felt as if every ounce of blood in her body were concentrated in her earlobes and her body was radiating heat like a stove. Her breasts were heaving in an effort to fill oxygen-starved lungs.

"Katherine?" the landlady asked cautiously in a quivering voice. When neither Katherine nor the handsome stranger answered, she began backing up and then ludicrously made a mad dash for the telephone in the living room.

The sight of Happy's bulk bouncing toward the telephone roused Katherine from her stupor. "Happy," she called and rushed after her landlady. She put a restraining hand on her friend's arm. "It . . . it's okay. Nothing's wrong. You just startled us, that's all."

"Well, you scared me to death!" Happy exclaimed.

"I'm not used to seeing strange men in your house, Katherine." She laughed and her chest and stomach shook. Her round face was wreathed in a genuine smile as she crossed to Jace and extended her hand. "I'm Happy Cooper, Katherine's friend and landlady. How's my angel doing?" she asked, indicating the sleeping Allison. "Isn't she the dearest baby you've ever seen? I love her like my own."

Jace shook the hand presented him and stared at Happy, overcome by her size and open friendliness.

"Katherine, introduce me to this beautiful man before I swoon. He looks like a movie star! Who is he?" Happy had never mastered prudence or tact. When she thought something, she said it.

Katherine groped for a plausible lie and stammered a near truth. "This . . . this is my . . . uh . . . brother-in-law. Yes. My late husband's brother and Allison's uncle."

She looked at Jace over Happy's gray coiffure and hoped that he had gotten the message. Would he give her away? She had loved the apartment on sight and wanted to rent it right away. Happy's initial hesitancy to lease it to a single woman with a baby had made it expedient for Katherine to invent a husband who had been killed. Most people couldn't deny anything to a young, helpless widow.

"What a pleasure, Mr. Adams," Happy gushed. "I'm sure Katherine feels reassured to have one of her family visit her."

"My name isn't Adams, Mrs. Cooper. It's Jason Manning. Jace."

Happy's cheerful countenance collapsed in bemusement. "Well, how is it that you and your brother have different names?"

Katherine held her breath and closed her eyes. Jace would expose her lie, and she would lose her most valued friend.

"He . . . he was only my half brother. We had different fathers," Jace lied smoothly. Did deception always come so easily for him?

"Oh, I see, of course," Happy patted Jace's hand. "It was a tragedy for him to die overseas like that. In Africa, wasn't it?"

Jace raised his eyebrows in a mocking, silent query and Katherine flushed. That he had been in Africa never entered her mind. It was just the most remote place she could think of as she told Happy a tale of an airplane crash that killed a nonexistent husband.

"Yes, Africa," said Jace. "And it was tragic. A pity he can't be here with us today." His face and voice were serious, but his blue eyes were glinting with humor as he looked at Katherine over Happy's head, which was bent as she dabbed her eyes with a lace-bordered handkerchief.

"Poor Katherine," Happy sighed as she once again turned to the young woman. Her look of concern was instantly converted to one of joy as she exclaimed, "But now that Jace is here, you won't have to go to the dance tonight alone. Isn't that lucky?''

She grabbed Jace's hand and shoved him toward Katherine.

Despite Jace's size, Happy's gentle push provided enough impetus for him to collide into Katherine. He reached out and grabbed her around the waist before she fell backward. They stared at each other, their faces close as he pulled her back to her feet. The kiss of moments before was still imprinted on their minds. Neither had taken it lightly.

''Here I was worrying about Katherine having to go unescorted to a dance, and right out of the blue a handsome brother-in-law drops in.'' Happy continued chattering happily, oblivious to Katherine's covert signals that she cease.

''Dance?'' Jace picked up on the idea. Did he have a radar device in his head?

''Yes! The faculty banquet and dance is tonight. Katherine's worked so hard on the arrangements. She's required to attend because of her job, and was having to go alone. Now you can take her. Do you have a tuxedo? Well, no matter. A dark suit will do just as nicely.''

''Happy, you don't understand. Mr. . . . uh . . . Jace isn't staying. He just came by—''

''Of course I'm staying, Katherine. Do you think I'd leave you stranded without an escort for this evening.

37

Besides I hadn't had time to tell you that the oil company I work for is drilling near here. I'll be around for a long time.''

Katherine stared open-mouthed at this announcement, but Happy clapped her hands in glee. "Oh, Jace, you can't imagine how happy that makes me. I never like to think that a young woman is left so alone in the world. It will be such a comfort to Katherine for you to be here.''

Jace was smiling benignly at Happy, but then he turned to Katherine. He impaled her with his eyes, and the message was clear. He was staying until he got custody of Allison.

"I've got to go now and carry my groceries in. I had just come in from shopping when I saw that cute little . . . uh . . .'' For once, Happy was at a loss for words.

"Jeep.'' Jace supplied.

"A jeep! How quaint!'' Happy chirped. Katherine rolled her eyes heavenward. Apparently Happy wasn't aware that the big status symbol these days was a four-wheel drive vehicle. "You two have a nice visit. I'll keep Allison tonight and you can stay out as late as you want to.''

"I've got to go for now too. Katherine, what time do I need to pick you up?'' Jace settled one large hand on her shoulder in brotherly affection, and, in deference to Happy's curious eyes, she stifled the impulse to fling it off. Things were moving too fast. She couldn't think. How could she spend an entire evening with him?

"Seven thirty," she heard herself answer and wasn't even conscious of shaping the words in her mouth.

"Okay, then. Happy, can I carry your groceries in for you? A lady like you shouldn't be doing menial tasks like that."

Happy giggled like a young girl. "Oh, Jace, I miss having a man around to do things like that. I really do. My son, Jim, lives . . ."

Her voice trailed off as they descended the stairs to the lawn below. Jason Manning. He was disgustingly transparent. He was being charming and a perfect gentleman. Was it his intention to get to her through her friends? What was his game plan?

He frightened her. He thrilled her. She must have been insane to even let him come into the house. A Manning wasn't to be trusted. Hadn't she seen how shallow Peter Manning's charming veneer was? She must protect Allison. But how? Jason Manning was too handsome and glib. Katherine thought these characteristics were far more formidable than malicious meanness and disreputability.

🌿❈ 🌿❈

The reflection in the mirror verified that Katherine's efforts in dressing for the dance hadn't been time wasted. She had soaked in a tub of bubble bath while Allison took her afternoon nap. The warm water was intended to ease some of her tension. Instead it had only made her more aware of the effect Jace's embrace had had on her body. She dried herself quickly, skimming over the most sensitive areas that continued to throb whenever she thought of his kiss.

Taking out the electric curlers, she began styling her hair. What should she have expected of Peter's brother? Peter had made a pass at her. He and Mary were already engaged.

One evening he had been waiting with Katherine for Mary to come downstairs. Katherine called up to her sister to hurry her along, uneasy being left alone with Peter even in her own house.

"You don't like me very much do you, Katherine?" he surprised her by asking. "Why not?" he insisted bluntly. "I'm quite charming when one gets to know me. I'd like for us to be friends."

He stood close behind her while she nonchalantly continued to water a plant near the window. His hand caressed her shoulder lightly. Her poise vanished at his touch. She turned quickly to face him, jerking his hand away.

"I don't know what you mean, Peter," she said sharply. "I don't know you well enough to say if I like you or not."

"Precisely my point!" he exclaimed, flashing her the famous smile that had been captured time and again in the society page photographs.

He reached out and put his hand under her elbow, squeezing it gently. "Why don't you and I have lunch

sometime soon, and''—his eyes lowered to her lips—
''get to know each other better.''

She shuddered in revulsion as his body moved closer
to hers. Loathingly she pushed him aside just as they
heard Mary coming down the stairs.

Mary was blissfully unaware of his personality flaws,
and, of course, Katherine never told her of the incident.
Even then he had been playing his macabre games.

At the lavish wedding reception he insulted Katherine
with another pass. Mary was chattering gaily to some
of the Mannings' friends when Peter sauntered over to
his new sister-in-law. She was making herself as invisi-
ble as possible amid potted plants and baskets of flowers.

''Sister Kate, how lovely you look in your bridal
frock.'' She hated that cooing voice and had learned to
dread it. He had adopted the nickname for her after she
rejected his first advance. It rankled her every time
he used it, but she would never have given him the
satisfaction of letting her anger show.

He took possession of her hands and kissed her coolly
on the cheek. She jumped back in mortification when
she felt his warm tongue poke through his lips and
lightly brush her cheek. His back was turned to the room
full of wedding guests, so no one had seen what he did.
The embrace appeared to be a filial kiss between new
in-laws.

She glared at him through slitted green eyes, but he
only smiled at her sardonically, his lip curled into a

smirk which marred the perfection of his regular features.

"You're unspeakably vile," she said.

"Tsk, tsk, sister Kate. Is that any way to talk to your dear brother?"

Justifiably she had hated Peter Manning.

"Yes, Mr. Jason Manning is running true to form and upholding the family traditions," Katherine said to her image as she misted herself with cologne.

Katherine critically scrutinized her gown and was pleased with what she saw. At the last moment she had decided to pack it when she left Denver. "I couldn't have afforded another one," she muttered ruefully. She had splurged on the expensive dress for a pre-wedding party at the Manning estate. It made a large dent in her budget, but it was worth it. The style was classic and would be in fashion for a while yet.

The sea-green georgette crepe draped close to her body and hung in soft folds at her feet. In a Grecian style, one shoulder was left bare while, on the other, the fabric was gathered into a graceful knot.

The dress accented her slender figure and clung to her gentle curves. The color flattered her summer's tan and brought out the highlights of her green eyes. Katherine was unconscious of how beautiful she looked in the dress. But she felt an added streak of confidence when she wore it.

She dropped her earring when she heard the knock on the door. Making one hasty last inspection, she retrieved the pearl cluster, inserted it into her pierced ear, secured the back, and went through the living room to answer Jace's knock.

Earlier in the day she had cleaned up the painting mess and moved the chest of drawers to the other bedroom. The living room was softly lit by shaded table lamps. Katherine hated overhead lights and glaring bulbs.

She opened the door and involuntarily caught her breath at the sight of Jace in his dark gray suit. From the distinctive buttons, she knew that it sported a designer label, and the European cut fit his physique perfectly.

His shirt was pale blue silk and his necktie a deeper shade of the same color. The wavy black hair had been brushed but still looked a trifle untamed. It shone with iridescent highlights.

He whistled long and low as he came through the door. "Wow! Can this be the same Widow Adams that I met this afternoon?"

"Come in, Mr. Manning." She hadn't missed his sarcasm. These games must stop if she were ever going to gain control. "Why are you doing this?" she asked in desperation.

"What?"

"This!" she cried, spreading her arms wide with palms up to encompass the whole situation. "Why are you being so pleasant and prolonging the inevitable confrontation? We both know why you're here, so I wish you'd drop this protective brother-in-law routine.''

He smiled but chided her softly. ''Remember who made up that ridiculous brother-in-law story, Katherine. Not I. I saved your skin today. You should be thanking me. Besides all that, I *am* your brother-in-law.''

''Oh!'' she ground out, clenching her fists at her sides. When she saw that he was not to be provoked, it angered her even more. ''Don't do this!'' she shouted.

A spark of annoyance flickered across his face and he put both hands on his hips. ''Look, all I'm here for is to take you to this dance, or whatever the hell it is. Is that so dastardly? Believe me, Katherine, I can think of several other ways I'd rather spend an evening with you.'' He fixed her with a warm blue stare and added suggestively, ''Shall I elaborate?''

For a moment, she was lost in the depths of his eyes, but she managed to answer hoarsely, ''No. Let's just get this over with. I'll get Allison.''

She went into the baby's room and was surprised when he followed her. ''Here, I'll carry her.'' He leaned toward the crib and reached for the baby.

''No,'' she said in a panic and grabbed his arm, drawing it away from Allison.

The face turned on her was angry, but softened when he saw the genuine fear in her eyes. ''I'm not going to run off with her, Katherine. That's not my style.'' Was that a censure for her leaving Denver with Allison? "I just wanted to carry her for you so she wouldn't wrinkle your dress. Okay?"

She licked her lips, ashamed of her outburst, and began gathering disposable diapers and putting them in a tote bag. "Okay," she conceded.

Jace gently turned the baby over onto her back and studied the pink, round face. He chuckled. "Say, you'll be a real beauty some day, Allison." His large hands were amazingly competent and gentle as he wrapped her in a light blanket and picked her up. He held her correctly, supporting her head in one of his palms. "She looks like—"

"Mary," interrupted Katherine quickly. She didn't want him to say that the baby looked like Peter.

He glanced at her over the baby's head. "That's what I was about to say. Of course, I never saw Mary, only pictures, but Allison has her coloring. Are her eyes blue? She's so lazy, she hasn't opened them for me yet."

Katherine laughed. "She's a good sleeper. And her eyes are blue. I hope they don't change color."

He turned to leave, but Katherine halted him. "Wait. She may spit up on your coat. Let me put this over your shoulder."

She picked up an absorbent pad and placed it over his shoulder, patting it into place. The close contact with his tall frame made her heart begin to pound. She stepped back quickly, but not before he noticed her reaction.

To cover her embarrassment, she busied herself with gathering up other supplies for the baby and switching out lights as they made their way out of the apartment.

Happy greeted them at the back door of her house and Jace relinquished Allison to her eager arms. She barely took the time to compliment them on how nice they looked before she began gurgling to Allison.

Crossing the lawn under the pecan trees, Jace suggested that they take her car. "I'm sorry, but the jeep is rather unsuitable for a date."

"No, we can take my car." She handed him the keys, and he clasped her elbow as he helped her into the passenger side. Her arm tingled long after his touch. The compact car barely accommodated his height, but somehow he managed to wedge himself behind the steering wheel, muttering deprecations and curses when he bumped first his head then his knee.

Planning the dinner-dance had consumed much of Katherine's time since her employment in the public relations office. Now it all seemed so inconsequential. All of her senses were absorbed by Jason Manning.

She made polite introductions; she ate dinner; she applauded the speaker; she conversed when she was required to. But everything paled against her awareness of the man beside her. Even among strangers he behaved with courtly manners and easy charm, totally confident of himself.

An awkward moment came when Katherine introduced Jace to her boss, Ronald Welsh. The two men eyed each other warily, and their immediate reciprocal hostility made Katherine uneasy.

"Mr. Welsh," Jace said as he extended his hand.

Ronald Welsh shook Jace's hand, but there was no warmth in his expressionless gray eyes as he murmured a greeting.

"Katherine, you look lovely this evening," he said, dismissing Jace and turning his full attention to Katherine. He reached out and stroked her arm. Instinctively she shrank away from him. Recently he had made similar moves in the office, and they never failed to make her uncomfortable. She didn't want him touching her. Unwarranted and unnecessary familiarity had always disturbed her. She reflected on the kiss this afternoon and pushed the thought aside. That hadn't been the same thing at all!

"Thank you, Ronald." He had insisted she call him by his first name, but she didn't like doing so. It altered their relationship in a manner that she felt was injurious to a professional rapport.

"Would you dance with me, Katherine?" Before she could answer, Ronald Welsh had scooped her into a bearlike embrace and hustled her away. There was little she could do but go along with him. After all, he was her boss, and she couldn't afford to offend him.

Ronald's thinning hair was heavily oiled in order to keep the sparse strands in place over the balding spots. The hair oil's perfume was overpowering.

"This is nice, isn't it?" he asked, drawing her closer to his short, thick body.

"Yes, very," she said. He seemed intent on holding her suffocatingly close and pressing her into his paunch.

She suffered through that dance and several others before Jace came up behind her and tapped her on the shoulder. He didn't issue a verbal invitation to dance. Instead one strong arm slid around her waist while the other captured her hand.

Jace pulled her close to him and led her into a slow, effortless dance. He didn't speak. She couldn't have. The sensations that were emanating from the pit of her stomach and spreading over her body reached her vocal cords, constricted them, and rendered them useless.

The hand that held her to him with fingers spread out wide on her back was like a brand that scorched her skin. Through the sheer fabric of her dress she could feel hard, muscular thighs pressing against her own. The warm breath that fanned her temple was soft and aromatic.

She was too close to him to look up into his face, but she could see the black curls that brushed his collar, and she had a compelling desire to slide her hand toward those curls and caress their black silkiness with her fingertips.

The music stopped and yet he didn't release her. He maintained a possessive hold on her arm and steered her to one of the French doors that led out onto a terrace.

Chapter Three

❧ ❧

The campus was dark. Only the banquet hall where the faculty dance was being held was lit. Katherine followed Jace's lead, never pausing to examine why she did so without any hesitation.

They crossed the brick terrace and a narrow strip of manicured lawn to a low wall that surrounded a rose garden. Before she could protest, he grasped her around the waist and swung her up to the top of the wall and sat her down. "Your feet hurt."

Could he read her mind? "How did you know? Was I limping? These are new shoes and they are killing me," she confessed.

"I saw you slip out of them just before I danced with you. I almost lost the heart to ask you but was afraid that if I didn't seize my chance, I may not have another with the belle of the ball," he teased.

"I'm hardly that," she protested. She started to remind him that he hadn't actually *asked* her to dance, but then his next action made her gasp.

He reached up under her long skirt and took one of her ankles between his warm palms. He slipped the uncomfortable high-heeled sandal off her slender foot and began massaging it with his long, strong fingers.

He grinned at her, ignoring her initial reflexive movement to take her foot away. His strokes were slow and rhythmical. "Dr. Manning's Famous Footrub. People come for miles to have one of these foot massages from me. Usually they have to wait for months for an appointment, but for you, little lady, I'll make a special deal."

His lighthearted mood was infectious. When had she last been able to relax and laugh? His medicine-man inflection was pure silliness, but she asked with mock seriousness, "Why am I suddenly afraid to hear the terms of this special deal?"

He raked her body with his eyes. He started at the top of her head and took in every feature of her face before moving to her throat and chest. His eyes lingered there for long moments before moving to her face again.

"You should be afraid," he whispered and brazenly winked at her.

She shifted, uncomfortable under his intent perusal. He released one foot only to grasp the other one and give it the same soothing treatment. His fingers were strong, but his caress was gentle.

They were quiet and the silence contributed to the unexpected intimacy. Nothing had ever stirred Katherine more than having Jace's hands under her skirt touching her with this exciting familiarity.

Was the forbidden, the unseen, always better? Is that why men of the last century couldn't resist a brief glimpse of a woman's ankle? Had modern women taken a giant step backward by flaunting their sexuality?

It was difficult to concentrate on anything while his thumb stroked her arch so sensuously, but she knew the subject of Allison still lay between them. Though, selfishly, she wanted this moment to go on forever, she couldn't remain silent. She cleared her throat and then asked bravely, "Jace, what are you going to do about Allison?"

His hands stopped their massage immediately, but he retained his hold on her foot. "What do you think I'm going to do?"

She swallowed hard and tried to control the trembling of her lips and the choked feeling in her throat. "Are you going to leave me alone with her?"

Quietly he answered her. "No, Katherine, I'm not."

She sobbed brokenly and jerked her foot from his startled fingers. She jumped off the wall before he had time to assist her and knelt down and fumbled in the damp grass trying to locate her shoes.

"Katherine, please don't," he said. Determined hands encircled her waist and brought her upright to face him. She struggled against him, but he refused to loosen his strong hold. His strength won out, and, finally, she ceased her efforts to escape and slumped against him in defeat.

His hands slid up and down her upper arms. Slowly he drew her closer to him until she was pressed against his long, hard body. He lowered his head and nuzzled the hair next to her cheek. With skill his fingers released the decorative comb which held back one side of her heavy hair. As it fell softly onto his face, he made a low, deep sound in his throat.

His fingers stroked her neck. Light kisses were brushed across her cheek as he rested his hand on her bare shoulder, caressing her collarbone with his thumb.

Katherine was incensed that he should take such liberties with her. Why wasn't she pushing him away? She never allowed a man such access to her. Any man.

But she was incapable of moving, of protesting. The heat of his body held her like a magnet. Her limbs were powerless to pull away. She wanted to take in more of the brisk, clean scent of his cologne. It was so easy to lean against his large, masculine frame and surrender to this floating sense of delicious vulnerability.

Could he feel her heart pounding under his hand? His hand! How had it gotten there? All of his motions felt so right, so good, she hadn't even noticed this caress that shocked her with its boldness.

He settled his lips against her mouth and breathed her name. "Katherine." His hand moved even lower from her bare shoulder, and he fit his palm over her breast. She pushed him away violently and struggled to regain her breath.

"Yes, you're a Manning," she cried in anger.

He was stunned, then defensive. "You make the name sound like an epithet."

"That's how I meant it," she snarled. All of her frustrations and worry over the last few hours poured into her words, and she lashed out at him viciously. "Your brother made a pass at me after he was engaged to my sister and with no encouragement from me. He did something even more obscene at his own wedding."

She shuddered as she remembered the feel of Peter's tongue on her cheek. The image of Jace doing the same thing was projected on her mind, and the picture wasn't at all repulsive. Impatiently she shoved the thought away and rasped in anger, "Now you come on to me panting and pawing. Do you think that a few soft caresses and sweet words will weaken my resolve? I will keep Allison and never let you or anyone else take her away from me. Do you finally understand? Stay away from her—and me." She was backing away from him, but it was a retreat from herself too. Even now she longed to return to the sensuous serenity of his arms.

She ran to her car and, after trying to open the door, realized that he still had the keys. Jace walked toward her slowly. Without speaking, he unlocked the door and held it for her. He made no move to touch her. When he had folded himself behind the wheel, he handed her the sandals which had been forsaken on the campus lawn.

They drove to her apartment in complete silence. He handed her the car keys, and she ran up the stairs without waiting for him to escort her. It was prearranged that Allison would stay all night with Happy.

Katherine slammed the door and locked it. Her hands covered her face as she leaned against the door, breathing hard and grappling with her conscience. She had let him kiss her. Twice. She had wanted to go on kissing him. And he was her enemy.

It was long after Katherine heard the jeep roar to life and speed down the street that she felt capable of leaving the support of the door.

※ ※

All night she tossed and turned, pounding her pillow and alternately folding her covers neatly over her and then kicking them to the foot of the bed. Katherine was furious with Jace for reducing her to this hot and bothered creature who was behaving like a teenager in the throes of her first big infatuation.

In actuality, that wasn't far from the truth. Since her father's death when she was a child, Katherine's life had been totally devoid of a masculine influence. No uncles, grandfathers, brothers, or male cousins were available to her, or her mother, or Mary.

Her natural apprehension toward men had increased during her adolescence and early adulthood. Contemporary mores relating to sexuality allowed men to demand more than she was willing to give. She was unprepared to handle such situations, and had subconsciously built a self-protective wall around herself. It had never crumbled.

Until today.

Why, when she was wary toward any man, had one so supremely masculine been able to arouse her like Jace Manning had? After being with him today she was resentful of this protection she forced on herself.

Just the thought of his long, lean body made her flush hotly. She tossed her head to the other side of the pillow as she recalled his cerulean eyes raking slowly over her body. Her skin still burned where his brown fingers had stroked it lingeringly.

She was more than a little afraid of him and what his unexpected intrusion could mean to her life and Allison's. Her physical and emotional reaction to him made the threat even more ominous. He was too big, too virile, too arrogant. Was he always so coolly confident?

And she despised his name. Manning. Manning. Peter Manning's brother. Peter, who had killed Mary with cruelty and thereby orphaned Allison. Peter, who used money and charm as facades to hide the decay in his soul.

She searched for traces of deception in Jace's face. His image was clear on the back of her burning, gritty lids. All she saw were two captivating blue eyes, deep dimples, and a sensuous, smiling mouth. With that picture fixed in her mind, she eventually dropped off into a restless slumber.

�*/🌟*

"Good afternoon, ladies!" Jace called as he hopped out of the jeep.

Katherine was sitting with Happy under the pecan trees in the backyard sipping cold homemade lemonade. They were interrupted by the squeal of brakes and the crunching of gravel under tires as Jace wheeled the mud-splattered jeep into Happy's driveway.

"Hello," cried Happy cheerfully and jumped out of her lawn chair to pour Jace a glass of lemonade from the pitcher on the glass-topped table nearby. "We're so glad you came by. We went to church this morning, but couldn't wait to get out of our girdles—well, of course,

Katherine never wears such a thing—and come out here and enjoy the breeze.''

Happy handed Jace the frosted glass. He thanked her profusely, but his eyes were glittering with mirth over the top of the glass as he raised it to his lips. He was appraising Katherine's figure, assessing whether she needed to be corseted or not. She blushed in embarrassment and looked down at Allison who was lying in her lap.

"Doesn't this child ever wake up?" Jace squatted down beside Katherine's chair and gently nudged Allison in the stomach. Katherine could feel his breath on her bare legs and was uncomfortably aware of his chest pressing against her calf.

"There you are!" exclaimed Happy as Allison lazily opened her eyes and inspected her uncle for the first time. As with all babies, Allison seemed attracted to a deep, soothing, masculine voice and studied Jace carefully as he talked softly to her.

"She's a beauty, isn't she?" he asked rhetorically, obviously impressed with the baby.

"Certainly she is," confirmed Happy. "Just look at her mother."

Confused for a moment before remembering Katherine's deception, Jace then turned to her and smiled in a disturbingly private way. "I see what you mean, Happy," he said. Then he bounced up, startling Allison who whimpered. "I'm sorry there, darlin', I didn't mean to scare you." He laughed. "I'll learn to be more careful around you."

Katherine cringed. He was still planning to be with Allison all the time. "Maybe you shouldn't come so close to her," she said nastily.

"But I *want* to be close to her," he replied matter-of-factly. He and Katherine stared at each other for a long moment.

Happy, who was inspecting her flower bed and missing the undercurrents between them, asked with innate curiosity, "Are you going swimming?" It was impossible not to notice that Jace was wearing only swimming trunks and an open-weave T-shirt.

Jace drew his eyes away from Katherine's and said cheerfully, "Yes, I came to see if Katherine and Allison would accompany me to the lake. The weather's mild enough for the baby, and the outing would be good for both of them I think."

How like him, Katherine thought. He wouldn't just call and ask her. He suggested it in front of Happy, who jumped at the idea enthusiastically. She hurriedly went into her kitchen to prepare them a snack to take along.

As soon as Happy was out of earshot, Katherine said, "I can't take a four-month-old baby into that lake and you know it."

"Okay," he said amiably, "I'll go swimming and you and Allison can relax in the shade."

"I'll have to get her ready." Katherine stood up and headed for her apartment.

"Un-uh," Jace said, grabbing her arm. "You'll go up there and discover some reason to prevent our going. How ready does a baby have to get? That's her diaper bag, isn't it?" He indicated the tote bag that had been taken to church that morning and was now lying on one of the lawn chairs. "We'll be back before she has to eat again."

"And how, pray tell, do you know what her feeding schedule is?" taunted Katherine.

"Lucky guess," he said, smiling that devastating smile that deepened the dimples on the sides of his mouth and crinkled the lines around his eyes.

Happy bustled out of her house carrying a basket. By the looks of it, they could eat out of it for at least a week. They climbed into the jeep. Katherine held Allison on her lap while Jace put the car bed on the back seat. He waved jovially to Happy as they pulled away.

The lake on the outskirts of town was man-made. Water from several rivers was channeled into it and the surrounding landscape had been turned into a public park which was an attractive spot to weekenders. Jace found a large shade tree on a grassy knoll away from the more crowded spots nearer the swimming area.

He retrieved a quilt from the back of the jeep and spread it out on the deep grass. He deposited the car bed for Allison on the quilt, then unselfconsciously peeled off his shirt.

The sight of his near-naked body was awesome. His trunks were navy blue with thin, red piping around the legs. The fabric was stretched taut across his flat abdomen. There was no line marking the border of his deep tan, and Katherine's cheeks were suffused with color over her speculation on how such a thing were possible.

"I'll be back soon. If you need me for anything, just yell real loud."

"Thank you, but we'll be fine," she answered politely.

He shot her an exasperated look before he loped down the hill toward the water. *Good!* She gloried in his annoyance. Maybe it would spoil this little expedition of his.

Allison was waving her arms and kicking her legs, excited and intrigued by the branches of the tree overhead. Katherine played with her until the baby got tired and started fretting. As soon as Katherine turned her over onto her stomach, she fell asleep.

"Killjoy," Katherine remarked ruefully as she stretched out on her back on the quilt. Involuntarily, she searched the lake, trying to distinguish Jace's head from the others that were bobbing up and down in the sun-gilded water. She threw her hands over her head, impatient with herself for caring where he was.

She was in that position, asleep, when Jace came back half an hour later. Katherine had forgotten how revealing her cotton knit tank top could be. It had to be worn braless, for the straps were thin. Her outstretched arms caused her nipples to press impudently against the soft fabric. The matching yellow shorts hid nothing of her long, slender legs, tanned apricot by the east Texas sun.

The sun found an opening in the thick foliage of the trees and shined onto her face. She blinked several times before allowing her eyes to open all the way.

At first she believed Jace's image to be an extention of a very pleasant dream, and her lips parted in an inviting, lazy smile.

She bolted upright when she realized he was no figment of her imagination. His black hair was still damp and several errant curls lay on his forehead. Nervously, she shifted her eyes away from his naked chest. It was covered with soft black hair that fanned across its broad expanse and tapered to a fine silky line on his stomach.

He reclined, stretching out his long legs and supporting himself on one elbow. He opened the basket Happy had provided and reached inside. "Apple? Orange?" he asked, holding up the pieces of fruit for her inspection.

"N-no, thank you," she stammered. His arm rested near her knee and his blatant virility completely unnerved her.

"Mind if I do?" He grinned as his strong, white teeth crunched into the apple. "Swimming always works up my appetite," he mumbled around the large bite. He concentrated on the apple for a few moments before he asked abruptly, "Like your work?" She had briefly outlined her job to him the evening before.

"Yes," she answered carefully, not sure where this

conversation was going to lead. "It's much more challenging than what I had done before. I'd still like to branch out into other kinds of writing though."

"Like what?"

Was he really interested, or was this his way of drawing her out, making her reveal secrets, failures? "I'd like to write copy for commercials, magazine ads, things like that."

He nodded, but didn't respond. "Do you like Mr. . . . uh . . . what's his name? Welsh?"

She shrugged. "He's all right, I guess. Sometimes I think he's a little strange, but then, he may think the same about me." Her attempt at humor flopped. Jace's face remained irritatingly noncommittal.

His uncharacteristic reticence made Katherine uneasy and she asked, "What do you do for the oil company? Drill for oil?"

"No. I try, sometimes with success, to *find* the oil. I'm a geologist for Sunglow."

"A geologist? I don't think I've ever known one before," she exclaimed, truly impressed.

"Would you like to get to know one better?" His eyes danced with a mischievous light as he covered her knee with his hand.

His move took her by surprise and for a moment she was too stunned to speak. Finally, in a voice not at all like her own, she asked, "How . . . how does one become a geologist?"

He laughed and removed his hand before answering.

"I studied in Arizona and New Mexico and Texas, too, at one time. Down near Houston. Much to my mother's horror, I did some research and experiments on an Indian reservation. I told her wild tales about scalping parties and war dances." He paused and winked at her slyly. "Actually, we only did rain dances."

She couldn't help laughing, thinking how Eleanor Manning, the queen of Denver society, would feel about her son living in close contact with Indians. Her laughter subsided and she grew serious. She gnawed at the inside of her cheek before asking, "How did you find me, Jace?"

"I found you to be beautiful, completely enchanting." His voice was tender and his words disconcerting, but they didn't deter her from her purpose.

"Please don't play games with me. I think Allison's future is too important."

He sobered instantly. "I'm sorry, and you're right." He sighed deeply and rolled over onto his back, clasping his hands under his head. "You covered your tracks well, Katherine. I had just about exhausted all possibilities when Elsie mentioned you and Mary. I was in my room at home, and she came in to clean. She started talking about Mary, and how sweet she was and how unhappy she'd been. Apparently they had developed quite a friendship. Anyway, she mentioned in passing that the only home Mary had ever known was Denver.

"Then she said, 'Of course, the girls were born in Texas.' I picked up on that and asked if she knew where.

She struggled to remember, and I nearly went out of my skull until she did.''

He breathed a deep sigh that expanded his ribcage and flattened his stomach. Katherine looked away quickly, alarmed that the motion had separated the waistband of his trunks from his skin.

He shrugged. ''I played a hunch and it paid off. It was a lucky break that Sunglow was going to be drilling in the east Texas oil field. I was here for three days before I presented myself at your door yesterday morning. You have been under surveillance, Miss Adams.'' He smiled up at her.

Her face was averted, looking toward the lake, so he continued quietly. ''Your house in Denver is sold. I tracked down the agent, and she's deposited the money from the sale into a savings account in Allison's name according to your instructions.''

''Good,'' Katherine replied.

Jace sat up then and asked, ''What did you live on, Katherine?''

She faced him and said defensively, ''If I had thought for one moment that I couldn't take proper care of Allison, I never would have taken her away from Denver.''

''I wasn't making an accusation.''

She pushed the honey-gold hair away from her face and said, ''I had a savings account with a couple of thousand dollars in it. We lived on that until I started receiving my paychecks from the college.''

''I'm sure you think you're capable of—''

"I *am* capable of taking care of her. I'm twenty-seven years old—"

"Twenty-seven?" he clamored. Allison stirred in her car bed and he lowered his voice to an incredulous whisper when he asked again, "Twenty-seven?"

"Yes. What's wrong with that?"

"Nothing," he laughed. "It's just that you look more like seventeen. I'm sorry. Continue."

After his outburst she couldn't remember what she had been saying. She collected her thoughts and went on. "I know I can earn enough to provide a comfortable home for Allison. It may not be as lavish as she would have had in Denver, but I love her." Her voice cracked with emotion. She couldn't give way now. She was fighting for her life.

"I have no doubt of that, Katherine. And you'll be able to provide a comfortable home. But have you thought about the future? What about college? Will you be able to provide that for Allison? And clothes? And all the thousand other things that a young, healthy girl needs?"

He was hitting too close for comfort. She had thought about those things and worried over them, but pushed them from her mind. Somehow, she would manage. She always had before.

"I give credence to what you're saying, Jace. It's a valid argument. But did you know that I put myself through college? I supported Mary after our mother died so she could go to school. I paid for most of her tuition, clothes, and so forth when she went to art school. I've taken care of myself for a long time, and I'm used to it.''

Her face was set determinedly as she returned his searching stare. He ran one hand across the back of his neck several times and, when he spoke again, he completely changed the subject. ''Is there anything to drink in there?'' he asked indicating the basket.

Katherine raised the lid and checked the contents. ''Let's see. We have root beer, root beer, and root beer,'' she enumerated as she took out one can at a time. She looked at him and laughed as he squinted his eyes in feigned indecision.

''I think I'll have a root beer,'' he stated, and they both laughed. She pulled the opener on the can and then shrieked as the drink spewed out and showered them both with the sweet effervescent liquid.

Hilarity overcame them, and it was several minutes before their laughter was spent. Jace was still chuckling as he studied her face and said, ''You're a mess.''

Wiping tears of mirth from her eyes, Katherine didn't resist when he pulled her up to her knees so that they were kneeling facing each other.

''Let's get some of this off,'' he said as he started stroking his fingers across her face and flicking drops of root beer to the ground.

In only moments Katherine was sensitive to a subtle change in his touch. Where before it had been quick and economical, it was now slow and caressing. She raised her eyes, not knowing that they were still wet with her recent happy tears and were most appealing.

Jace searched their green depths as his thumbs swept across her trembling lips. Moving slowly, he cupped her head in his palms, his fingers entwined in her tousled hair, and drew her face to his.

The lips that touched hers were warm and sweet and gentle, and, at first, tentative. But they became more demanding as his arms went around her and pressed her into his body.

She stiffened in resistance, and he sensed her withdrawal immediately. Without releasing her, his hold became more gentle. He stroked her back tenderly. His lips changed from demanding to persuasive. His tongue circled her closed lips, and he nibbled at a corner of her mouth. Against her will, Katherine felt her mouth relaxing under his until she moaned and accepted his ardent probing.

When they were both breathless, he pulled his mouth from hers, but gave fervent attention to her ears. He kissed her eyelids.

"Your eyes are the color of a new spring leaf." His whisper was deep and husky. "Where did you get these black lashes? Blondes don't usually have eyelashes this dark."

His hands and lips intently caressed each feature of her face. He ran his fingers through her hair. "Your hair is like cool silk. I want to feel it blowing across my face." He took her mouth with more precision than before, drawing responses from her that she had never given to anyone else.

One strong hand went to the small of her back and drew her even closer to him. His knees moved apart, making his stance wider, and she positioned her legs between his. She felt the strength of his long thighs as they pressed against hers.

The sensations coursing through her were frightening, and she would have pulled away, but the lips nuzzling her neck were gentle, and the hands stroking the satin skin of her back under her tank top were tender. There was no threat of danger, was there? Shyly she raised her arms and placed them around his neck, touching the muscles of his shoulders.

"Oh, God, Katherine." His voice was as urgent as his hands as they lifted the hem of her shirt. The hairs on his chest tickled her breasts and stomach as they were bared and pressed against him.

"Katherine, I want you." She couldn't ignore the evidence of his desire when they were this close to each other. "You're beautiful . . . sweet . . ."

His hand covered her breasts and somewhere in her head alarm bells sounded. She didn't behave this way! She should resist him. He was a Manning, and even if he weren't—

Oh! What was happening to her? Her nipples ached with desire as he caressed them. Katherine clenched her hands on his shoulders in awakening passion.

Please, no. Jace, Jace. No, Jace. Then Katherine

realized she was actually saying his name aloud and it was in the form of a sob. It mingled with his soft mutterings against her flesh.

"Katherine, you feel . . . Your breasts. Katherine, please—"

"No!" she screamed and pushed away from him, unbalancing him and making him fall backward. "No! Don't touch me." She hastily pulled down her shirt and covered her flaming cheeks with shaking hands.

"Katherine, I—"

"Don't . . . don't make any excuses. Just leave me alone." She was sobbing uncontrollably and didn't know why. Was it out of shame or a sense of loss? She couldn't afford to trace the source of her tears.

She unleashed the anger she felt toward herself on him. "Did you really expect me to let you . . . ? God, what was I doing?" As if cautiously retreating from something dangerous, she took several steps backward. "You expect everyone to cater to your whims. Was I supposed to be honored that a mighty Manning paid me some attention? And if I submitted, that would be more ammunition you could use against me. I remember what your lawyer said about my indeterminate morals. You're conceited and selfish and arrogant and deceitful. Just like your brother," she sneered and turned away from him.

Within a heartbeat he had gripped her upper arm painfully and spun her around to face him. The eyes that had been glazed with passion only moments before now blazed with fury. Gone were the deep dimples and the sensuous smile. In their place was a thin, grim slash of a mouth set in a granite-hard chin.

Katherine shrank from the latent violence that surfaced even as she watched. "Goddamn you! Don't ever say that to me again. Do you hear me?" He gave her a little shake and her head wobbled on her shoulders. "Never compare me to my brother. Never!" He said the last word through clenched teeth, and the cords in his neck stood out.

Katherine winced with pain from his death grip on her arm. That he was hurting her finally penetrated his anger, and he released her abruptly and stepped back. Pent-up breath was released in a great expulsion of air as the heels of his hands dug into his eyes.

When he looked at her again he said hoarsely, "Forgive me. I came on too strong."

Chapter Four

❧ ❧

Whether he was referring to coming on too strong sexually or his attack of violent temper, she never knew. He hastily began gathering their things and packing them into the jeep.

Katherine braved one quick look at him on the silent trip home. His jaw was set and hard, his eyes were fixed on the road. When they arrived at the house, she stumbled up the stairs to her apartment carrying Allison and leaving Jason to return Happy's basket and report on their outing.

The following morning she went to work as usual, but nothing was the same. The weekend had been tumultuous. She was nervous and edgy, jumping at her own shadow. Having no idea what Jace's next move was going to be was tormenting.

She didn't think he would try to steal Allison away from Happy's house while she was working, but then, she couldn't trust him not to. He didn't seem the type to do something so heinous, but Peter had shone with good intentions toward his wife too.

No, despite his charm and good looks, Jace Manning could not be trusted. She would be foolish to think otherwise.

It didn't take long for him to reveal his method of operation. When she came home from work, he was in the backyard with Happy helping her repair a window screen. He had his nerve!

"Wasn't it sweet of Jace to fix this old thing for me? All I had to do was mention that it was broken and nothing would do but for him to come out here and have a look at it."

"I'll just bet," Katherine mocked, but her sarcasm was lost on the unsuspecting Happy. Didn't she wonder what Jace's reason for coming around was in the first place?

Jace answered that question for her. "The roughnecks are doing some preliminary land clearing on the site where we want to drill, so I'm free for a few days. Isn't that fortunate?" His smile was beguiling and deliberately aggravating.

"Extremely," Katherine smiled back with matched

brilliance, hoping to provoke him. But he only laughed. He was the most infuriating man!

The next few days fell into the same pattern. He was everywhere. Every time Katherine turned around, Jace was there. He helped Happy with odd jobs; he took her car to be serviced; he sat with Allison one afternoon so Happy could attend a woman's social at the church. He offered to help Katherine in her apartment, but she summarily refused his smallest gesture of kindness. She wasn't going to be swayed by this hypocritical charade.

By Friday afternoon her nerves were frayed to shreds. With the fall semester starting, her office had been unusually busy. She wasn't able to keep up the writing of the press releases and promotional material that was required of her. Jace and his activities had weighed heavily on her mind all week, and she found it hard to concentrate while sitting at her typewriter.

"Katherine." She jumped as Ronald Welsh spoke at her shoulder. He had an annoying habit of sneaking up on her and then profusely apologizing for it. His comforting pats on the arm disturbed her.

It had been necessary to continue the lie about her being a widow when she applied for the job. He had been moved by her tragic story, and Katherine thought his immediate concern for a total stranger had been suspiciously effusive.

"Did I startle you? I'm sorry." As she placed the plastic cover over her typewriter, he came around to face her. "Are you in a hurry to leave tonight? hought maybe we could start celebrating the long weekend early with a drink?''

Katherine shrank from the large, beefy hand that had settled on her shoulder and pinned her to the chair. She tried not to panic or jump to the wrong conclusion, but suddenly she felt uneasy in the close intimacy of the office.

"Oh, thank you, Mr. Welsh—"

"Ronald."

"R-Ronald, but I really do need to get home. My goodness, look how late it is," she cried, making a cursory check on her wristwatch, and not even noting or caring about the time. She only wanted to leave the confines of the small office.

She managed to extricate herself from the chair, but as she moved toward the door, he grasped her arm. "Everyone else is gone, Katherine. They were all so anxious to clear out and get a start on the Labor Day holiday. We can have the building all to ourselves and enjoy our own celebration." To her increasing horror, he crossed to the door and locked it.

"I know you don't want to disappoint me. You like working here, don't you? I hope so. It's so important that you keep a stable job like this one. I mean, you're a widow with a little girl, you know," he cooed unctuously.

Katherine's throat constricted in fear as he stared at her with glinting, fevered eyes. She swallowed convulsively and decided that her best defense was bluffing him into thinking she was agreeable to his tête-à-tête.

"On second thought, Ronald. A drink sounds nice," she said brightly through frozen lips. Her whole face had become stiff. She had to get to that door!

"I knew you'd go along, Katherine." His short, thick body moved toward her, and he reached out and stroked her cheek with sausagelike fingers.

Katherine nearly choked on the bile that rose up in the back of her throat, but she managed a caricature of a smile. Her mouth was so dry that her lips stuck to her teeth.

"What do you like to drink, my dear? Did you know that I had this little liquor cabinet hidden here for occasions such as this?"

He winked at her before he turned around to lean over a desk drawer. Katherine took one hesitant step toward the door. To cover her movement she said, "Anything is fine with me. Whatever you're having."

"I love an uncomplicated woman." He straightened, holding a bottle of cheap liquor in one hand and two dusty glasses in the other. Katherine recognized them as those that were used in the campus cafeteria and wanted to laugh hysterically. Mr. Ronald Welsh didn't waste any money on his seductions.

"Come over here and sit beside me, Katherine. I want you to relax." He settled his bulky frame on the small sofa and patted the cushion.

Other than making a mad dash for the door which was across the room, Katherine had no choice. She would have to bide her time until she saw an opportunity for escape. But would such an opportunity come before it was too late? On shaky knees she went to the sofa and sat down beside him.

The sweet odor of the thick hair oil, his sweat, and the reeking liquor he was extending toward her almost made her retch. But she smiled and raised the glass to her lips. Her drinking habits were limited to wine or drinks that camouflaged the taste of liquor. She could barely swallow her tentative sip of the raw, burning rye.

"I like girls who wear dresses. You've never come to work in anything but a skirt or a dress." He placed his sweaty palm on her knee and began inching it up by small degrees. This couldn't be happening to her!

"A lot of men don't like panty hose, but I do. I find panty hose incredibly sexy, Katherine." His hand was under her skirt now, sliding higher and pressing harder. Beads of perspiration dotted his upper lip.

"Please, Mr. . . . Ronald—" Her voice came out high and squeaky. His next move took her completely by surprise.

He lunged at her, forcing her backward on the sofa. He fell on top of her, knocking the breath out of her. His heavy hand reached for the front of her silk shirt, and the breast pocket came away in his fist as she jerked out of his grasp.

"You can't fool me, Katherine. You want this as much as I do," he grunted. "Go ahead and scream if you want to. No one will hear you."

He was panting, or was that her own ragged breath that echoed in her head as she struggled under his crushing weight. "No . . . oh, God . . . you're mad . . . please, no."

He grabbed the front of her shirt and ripped it apart, sending buttons flying. He tried vainly to open the front clasp of her bra, but when his frantic fingers couldn't manage that, he impatiently broke the plastic fastener.

His mouth crashed down on hers. His thick lips pulled at hers, and, when she bit them, he raised one hand and slapped a stinging blow across her cheek.

Her tender breasts were exposed to his rough handling. Katherine cried out in pain as he scratched them and kneaded them with bruising pinches.

When his lips left hers to bury themselves in her neck, she screamed with her last ounce of strength. The piercing sound was joined with that of breaking glass and splintering wood.

Over Ronald Welsh's bulky shoulder, she saw Jace's booted foot give one final kick, and the door swung open under the impact. He was on Ronald in three long strides.

Grabbing the other man by the collar of his coat, Jace pulled him off Katherine and flung him into the opposite wall.

"You bastard!" Jace growled as he crammed his fist into Ronald's stupefied face. Katherine heard the sickening crunch of a nose breaking and saw blood spurt out of the smashed feature.

She sobbed hysterically as Jace continued to pummel Ronald's sagging body. He was no longer coherent and slowly slumped against the wall, supported only by Jace's grip on the front of his blood-splattered shirt.

Jace shoved his fist into Ronald's belly one last time and then let him go. With a deep, animal moan, Ronald collapsed into a heap on the floor.

Jace stood over the still form, his chest and shoulders heaving in exertion. He raked one sleeve across his forehead and then slowly turned toward Katherine.

She managed to sit upright, but felt that at any moment she was going to start screaming and never stop.

Jace knelt down in front of her and smoothed back the tangled hair from her white face. "Katherine?" he asked softly. "Katherine, are you all right?" His face was filled with such anxious concern that when she saw it, she was unable to contain the tears that flooded her eyes, and they spilled down her cheeks.

"Y-yes," she nodded. He wiped the tears away with his fingers and rested his palm against the red mark on her face. His lips formed a hard, grim line.

"I'll be right back. I want to get—" He made a motion to get up, but she clutched his shoulders with desperate hands.

"No! Please, Jace, don't leave me alone in here with

him. I can't stand it. Please.'' She was becoming hysterical and couldn't stem the flow of words.

Jace pulled her to him and cradled her head against his shoulder. He stroked the back of her head reassuringly.

"Hush, hush. It's okay. I won't leave you, Katherine. I promise. Hush now. I was only going to find something to write on. The president of this august institution is going to hear about this tonight. But I guess a telephone call will be even better.''

Jace maintained his hold on her as he drew her up. He balanced the trembling body against his as he picked up her purse on the desk, then swept her into his arms and carried her out of the building into the quiet evening. It was already dark and the campus of Van Buren College was deserted.

When he had her settled in the jeep, he fumbled through the myriad articles stashed in the back of it until he found what he was looking for.

"Here, Katherine, put this on.'' She recoiled from the hands that reached toward her ripped blouse which she clutched together in an effort to cover herself.

Patiently he stated his motive. ''Katherine, if Happy sees you like that, you'll have to make a lot of painful explanations. Slip into this T-shirt and maybe we can get you into the house without attracting her attention. If she comments on the shirt, I'll tell her you spilled ink or threw up or something. Okay?''

She nodded and didn't resist when he gently eased her out of the torn, ruined blouse. He tossed it to the floor of the jeep. Although cocooned as she was in apathy, Katherine blushed with embarrassment when he slid the straps of her bra from her arms.

"Goddamn him," he murmured when he saw the welts and bruises on the smooth breasts. With infinite tenderness, he touched one of the deeper scratches with his fingertip.

Katherine watched his face, incredulous that she should see such emotion there. The warmth of his hand was transmitted to her and his touch seemed to heal her from the physical pain of the assault and the emotional upheaval of the trauma.

Jace's teeth clenched and he hissed harshly, "I ought to go back and kill that sonofabitch!" Trying his best not to cause her more pain, he slipped the T-shirt over her head. It was far too large for her, but the soft cloth felt good.

When he was assured that she was comfortable, Jace straightened in his seat and started the jeep. He drove without undue speed, and, when they reached Katherine's yard, he cut the motor and got out of the jeep without speaking. Katherine noted with relief that Happy's car wasn't parked in its usual spot.

He didn't allow her any time to protest but carried her up the stairs. He looked at her inquiringly, and she indicated Allison's room.

He deposited her on the twin-size day bed that she slept on.

"What can I do to help?" he asked. "And don't give me that crap about not needing my help."

She looked up at him and her lips trembled as she gulped, "Th-thank you, Jace. He was going to . . . I don't know if I could have fought him much longer. It was terrible." She shuddered and folded her arms across her chest, holding herself tightly and rocking back and forth.

"God, Katherine, I can't even imagine how horrifying it was for you. When I went through that door and saw—"

"What were you doing there?" it suddenly occurred to her to ask.

He didn't meet her eyes as he answered in a mutter, "I . . . uh . . . ever since I met that . . . him at the dance, I've felt like something wasn't right. Intuition. The way he looked at you bothered me. I've been keeping my eye on him. When the building got dark and everyone left but the two of you, I got suspicious. I tried the door and found it locked. That's when you screamed."

"Thank you," she whispered and shyly reached for his hand. He grasped her small one in his and stared deeply into her eyes as his thumb traced a hypnotizing circle in her palm. The combination of his caress and his penetrating stare made Katherine uncomfortably warm and she forced herself to pull her hand from his. He released it immediately.

"I would like to take a bath," Katherine said.

"All right. You do that while I make some telephone calls." He went out and shut the door behind him.

The warm water stung the fresh scratches, but she felt cleansed of Ronald's smell and touch by the time she left the bathroom. She put on a cotton nightgown and climbed into the bed beside the crib.

"Coming through," Jace called before he eased into the room backward, using his bottom to open the door. He was carrying a tray with both hands. "Room service," he said cheerfully. Katherine laughed to see a tea towel tucked into the waistband of his jeans. He gingerly placed the tray on her lap and stood up, proudly inspecting his labors.

"I thought you might like some tea and toast. If you want an omelet or anything else, I'll fix it for you. I didn't think you'd want a heavy meal."

"This is perfect," she said taking a sip of the scalding tea.

Casually and without any hesitation, he sat down on the end of the bed and leaned back over her feet, supporting himself on his elbows.

"For your information, Mr. Ronald Welsh is no longer employed at Van Buren College. I called the president, interrupted a barbecue supper at his house, and told him the whole story. I threatened newspaper headlines and petitions against sexual harassment on the job if he didn't cooperate. He was easily convinced."

He smiled at Katherine, but there was no humor lighting the blue eyes.

"Mr. Welsh?" she asked timidly, remembering his crumpled body on the office floor.

"I called an ambulance for him," Jace said grudgingly.

Katherine nodded absently. "He has a family. I wonder what will happen to them when he loses his job," she mused.

"They'll be taken care of along with the hospital bill."

Katherine looked at him in surprise. "What do you mean?"

He picked up one of Allison's stuffed animals and studied its ears. "Never mind," he answered vaguely, then said quickly, "Someone from the college will bring your car home."

Before Katherine could question him any further, they heard Happy's cheerful call as she came through the front door in the living room. "Katherine, Jace, are you in here? Allison and I had an errand to run and I . . ." Her voice trailed off as her huge bulk filled the doorway.

Jace made no attempt to get up off the bed, and Happy's eyes opened in shock when she saw the two of them on the small bed and Katherine tucked in for the night.

"What—"

Jace didn't let her finish but stood up and relieved her of Allison.

"Katherine's tummy got a little upset at work. She called and asked me to come drive her home. I insisted that she get right into bed and get a good night's sleep."

He lied so glibly, Katherine thought.

"Oh, my dear, are you feeling all right? Maybe we should call a doctor," suggested Happy, and Katherine reacted instantly.

"No. No, I'm fine. I think I ate something at lunch that didn't agree with me."

"Jace is right. You stay right in that bed and don't worry about a thing. I'll take Allison back to my house for the night."

"No, Happy. I want her here with me," Katherine said. Somehow Allison's small body provided a sense of security and stability to her shattered nerves.

"But what if you have a contagious virus? The baby—"

"No, it's nothing like that." Jace interrupted Happy's objections. "I've decided to stay here tonight. If Katherine needs any help or starts feeling worse, I'll call for you."

Katherine and Happy both looked at him in astonishment. Happy was the first to recover. "But, Jace, are you sure that's proper. I mean—"

"Of course. I'll stay in the living room. I was going to be up all night going over some graphs and doing some charting anyway, so I'd just as well do it here."

Happy was reluctant to agree, but Jace's manner was so disarming that she stifled any further protests.

"I think we'd better let Katherine get to sleep," he hinted, and Happy quickly responded. She said a hurried good night, patted Allison on the back, and left.

Jace laid Allison in her crib and said, "Don't go away, princess, I'll be right back." He turned in the narrow space between the crib and the bed and asked, "Are you finished?" Katherine nodded affirmatively. "Want anything else?" She nodded negatively. He took the tray and went out of the room.

When he returned, he rubbed his hands together briskly and leaned over the crib. "I've never done this, Allison, but you can talk me through it, okay?"

Katherine laughed as his big hands grappled with the tiny buttons on Allison's playsuit. He finally got her out of it and changed her diaper, putting on a more absorbent disposable for the night. When she was properly creamed, powdered, snapped, and buttoned into pajamas, he lifted her out of the crib and carried her into the kitchen to get her bottle. Katherine could hear him talking to the baby the whole while.

He came back with the bottle of milk in one hand. He sat down in the wicker rocking chair and winced when he heard it crackling under his weight.

"Is this damn thing going to hold me?" he asked and Katherine laughed.

"I hope so," she said in a voice muffled by her covers.

"It's all Allison's fault, you know. If she weren't so fat, we wouldn't be so heavy. You hear that, princess? You're going to have to go on a diet." He plopped the bottle into her mouth and she smacked it eagerly with hungry lips.

From her bed Katherine watched Jace as he fed the baby. He talked to her softly, and she stared up at him in fixed fascination. Her tiny fists reached out for his face as he leaned down over her.

The warm tea in her stomach and the soothing sound of Jace's deep voice made Katherine drowsy, and she snuggled down deeper into the light covers, sighing contentedly.

When Allison had done justice to the milk in the bottle, Jace put her to his shoulder to burp her. He laughed when she produced a booming belch.

He laid Allison in the crib on her stomach and patted her round bottom before pulling a flannel blanket over her. Then he put out the lamp on the table next to Katherine's bed. Only the light from the living room filtered through the doorway into the dim room.

Jace sat on the edge of the twin bed and supported himself on hands place on either side of Katherine. "How are you?" he whispered.

She felt protected and young, as helpless and dependent as Allison. "I'm fine," she whispered back.

His breath stirred her hair as he lowered his head and brushed warm lips across her forehead. She closed her eyes and felt feather-light kisses on her lids. He trailed his lips to her ear and she accommodated them by turning her head on the pillow and allowing him access.

"I know you're in no mood for romance after the experience you had tonight, but, Katherine, I want so much to kiss you." He breathed the words in her ear, and she felt the moist tip of his tongue caress her earlobe.

With a small gasp of pleasure she turned her face toward his, searched for his mouth in the darkness, found it, and melted her lips onto his.

They thought each other to be delicious. Tasting was as much a part of the kiss as touching. He drove her mad with a darting tongue that wouldn't be caught until it had tickled each crevice of her mouth. Then it filled her mouth and she moaned, working her fingers through his hair and capturing his head even as she held his tongue.

"Katherine," he rasped against her cheek, "I can't do this for much longer."

"No?" she asked disappointedly.

"No," he replied shakily.

She reluctantly unlocked her hands from the back of his neck, and he started to stand. "Jace," she said.

He reseated himself beside her and answered huskily, "Yes?"

Timidly she reached out and slipped her hand into the opening of his shirt. She moved her fingers over the crisp hairs and smoothed the warm muscles. "Thank you again for what you did."

He groaned and leaned over her again. This time his mouth took hers with unleashed passion. His hand went under the covers and settled on her waist. She was aware of his every move through the thin cotton of her nightgown. His hand smoothed over her hip and then eased to her stomach. He pressed his fingers flat, covering her entire abdomen.

A current of pleasure mixed with fear knifed through her as his palm rested on the triangle between her thighs. The seconds ticked by in rhythm to Katherine's accelerated heartbeat. He didn't move except to continue his ardent kiss. Then slowly, almost imperceptibly, his hand began making small concentric circles over her. His fingers caressed lower and deeper until—

"Jace!" It was a cry of alarm, and he removed his hand immediately. He cupped her face between his hands.

"I won't bother you tonight. I promised myself I wouldn't. And I will never hurt you." He kissed her gently with closed lips and left the room, shutting the door behind him.

❦ ❦

The next morning Katherine wrapped a robe around herself and changed a fussy, hungry Allison before venturing into the other rooms.

Jace was at the kitchen sink, humming as he squeezed orange juice into a pitcher. The aroma of freshly brewed coffee filled the room. "Good morning, ladies," he said, glancing over his shoulder.

"Good morning. Did you get any sleep?" Katherine noticed several charts and graphs spread out on the living room floor.

"A few catnaps." He wiped his hands on a towel as he faced her. He dropped his bantering tone and asked, "How do you feel?"

She smiled at him and said firmly, "I'm fine, Jace. Really. It seems like a bad dream now in the light of day."

"Good. I'm glad." He stroked her cheek briefly then said, "You feed the princess and I'll fix us some eggs."

"All right," Katherine agreed. Just then the telephone rang and she reached to answer it. "Hello."

She handed the instrument to Jace with a puzzled look on her face. How had anyone known he was here? "Long distance and person-to-person for you," she said.

He didn't meet her eyes as he said brusquely into the receiver, "Jace Manning. Yeah, Mark. Oh, *damn!* Well, I thought they might . . . I don't know. Is everything all set? What's his name again? Okay, what time? No, but I'll find it. Hell, I forgot about the holiday. No. No. I thought they might try a trick like this. I will . . . Yeah. If there's anything else I should know, call me. You, too. When it's done, I'll call you. You can tell them. Yeah, it'll hit the fan, all right. Good-bye and thanks, Mark."

He hung up the wall phone and stared at it for long moments before he turned around to meet Katherine's wide, green, questioning eyes.

"How long will it take you to get ready to drive to Dallas?"

"Dallas?" she asked. "Why would I be going to Dallas?"

"For a wedding. We're getting married today."

Chapter Five

ave you lost your mind?"

Katherine choked on her question as she stared at Jace in incredulity. He met her shocked stare with a level one of his own.

"Probably," he said grimly, "but our options don't leave us much choice."

"Our options? What are you talking about?" Allison was growing more fretful each second. Katherine shifted the baby to her other shoulder and absently bounced her up and down. All her attention was focused on the man who, in a week's time, had assumed control of her life.

"Katherine." His calm voice was infuriating. "Why don't you get Allison's bottle and feed her while we talk."

Katherine shot him a deadly look, but she turned and picked up the bottle of milk he had had the foresight to take out of the refrigerator an hour earlier. She sat down in one of the bentwood chairs at the kitchen table and positioned Allison under her breast in the crook of her left arm. She would satisfy the infant's momentary fussiness with the bottle and feed her cereal and fruit later. Right now she couldn't risk being distracted.

With as much poise as she could muster, she asked, "Okay, who was that calling you on my telephone? I want to know *now* what you meant when you said that you and I were getting married. Mind you, there's not the slightest chance in hell that we are, I'm just curious as to how you arrived at such an absurd idea." Katherine felt that under the circumstances, her pronouncement was a masterpiece.

Jace grinned at her while he poured a cup of coffee and said, "Please watch your language in front of the baby, Katherine. How do you take your coffee?" He found that intensely humorous and laughed out loud, startling Allison who glanced at him over the bottle she was sucking at.

"Here I've just proposed marriage to a woman, and I don't even know how she drinks her coffee, or even if she does." He raised an arched brow in query.

"A drop of milk please," said Katherine. When was he going to get to the subject at hand?

He prepared her coffee and set it in front of her on the table. He refilled his own mug and straddled another chair, folding his arms over the curved back.

"Katherine, my parents are going to claim that you kidnapped their grandchild. They'll probably have you arrested if they can find you."

He allowed time for his words to sink in. Katherine's face drained of color. Allison squirmed as her aunt's arms suddenly clenched her tighter. She shook her head from side to side, denying what he said as truth.

"No, no, they can't! I have guardianship of her. My sister—"

He interrupted her. "They can and they will. Believe me. Let me start at the beginning, okay?" She nodded, unable to speak, and he told her what he knew of the situation in Denver.

"A friend of mine, a lawyer, has been keeping tabs on things. When I got back from Africa, I found my parents to be upset with you to say the least. They were making all kinds of threats even then. They want Allison."

When he saw that she was about to comment, he held up his hand. "Hear me out, okay?" Reluctantly, she nodded and he continued. "Just about the time I left to come here, they were talking about kidnapping, the FBI, the whole ball of wax. I told Mark—my friend—

to let me know when he heard something definitive. I've been checking with him every few days and gave him your number in case he couldn't reach me through Sunglow or at the motel.''

"But I didn't kidnap her, Jace,'' Katherine exclaimed when he paused to draw a breath and sip his coffee. "Mary gave her to me before she died. I have a paper to prove it.''

"Where is it?'' he asked.

She hesitated then indicated a desk in the living room. "Third drawer on the left.'' If he should destroy the document, she still had the original in the safety deposit box in Denver.

He got the copy out of the desk and returned to his chair in the kitchen. He scanned the paper, then raised sad eyes to Katherine.

"She wrote this just before she died?''

"Yes,'' Katherine confirmed hoarsely.

"It's eloquent and puissant, but I doubt if it would hold up in a court of law, Katherine.''

"I have the original safe in Denver,'' she added hopefully.

"Even so,'' he shook his head and sighed. "Did anyone witness her writing this? No one else signed it.''

Katherine shook her head dispiritedly. "No,'' she said.

"Each state has its own criteria for the legality of handwritten wills. We could check into the Colorado stipulations but . . .'' He shrugged as his voice trailed off. He made a tent with his fingers and rubbed them over the tip of his nose as he studied her. "Katherine, let me tell you what I've arranged." He stood up and walked to the sink, staring out at the morning landscape from the square window.

"From past experience, it was reasonable for me to assume that my parents would take drastic measures to get custody of Peter's baby."

It was the first time that name had actually been spoken between them. Reminders of Peter could still cause Katherine to shiver in revulsion. Would the image of Mary's pale, haggard, unhappy face ever be erased from her mind? Jace brought her out of her reverie instantly.

"I meant to get custody of Allison myself. That's why I came looking for you." He glanced at her briefly over his shoulder. "You were right to be wary of me when I first arrived. I had every intention of taking you to court if necessary to get Allison. But then . . . you . . . well, anyway, I saw how good you were with her, and I know that an infant needs a mother. So"—he shrugged—"I started thinking that we should combine our efforts and share her. I had Mark make the necessary arrangements for us to obtain a Texas marriage license. He has a buddy in the Dallas County Court House. And now, since Mother and Dad are making real their threats, I think we should get married as soon as possible. Today."

She couldn't believe he was taking charge of her

life so blithely, not even considering that she might object.

"Well, Mr. Manning," she said, "I'm not ready to marry you or anyone else. And if you think I'd ever marry a Manning, you're crazy. I haven't forgotten Peter's cruelty to Mary. There's no question of my forgiving it."

He spun around and faced her. "Look, I know how you feel about my family and I know why. I can't say that I blame you for that."

"Thank you," she retorted sarcastically. "How do I know that this isn't all some set-up? You could still take Allison away from me and give her to your parents. I find it hard to believe that some roughneck, no matter how nobly he pleads his case, really wants responsibility for a four-month-old baby."

Her words were mean and ugly, but so were the circumstances. She was breathing hard in her consternation. If it weren't for Allison, she would have stood and faced him head-on. "Do you know what Allison will grow up to be under the influence of your mother? She—"

"Yes," he said calmly amid her tirade. "I know."

She was momentarily taken aback. "Yes?"

"She'll be silly and stupid and care nothing for anyone or anything except herself. Just like her father."

Katherine opened and shut her mouth several times before she could say anything. "I'm sorry. I didn't—"

"Please don't apologize. It clears up the matter for

me. You obviously have a very low opinion of me. You see me as no different from them. No wonder you think our marriage is already on rocky ground.''

''I'm *not* going to marry you, Jace!'' she shouted. Then she lowered her voice and said, ''I was taught that marriage is a permanent condition and there's no—''

''Being indicted for kidnapping is a permanent condition too, Katherine. Wait a minute,'' he barked when she started to object. ''I don't think they could make such a charge stick either, but the stigma would be with you for the rest of your life. Peter's and Mary's deaths, not to mention that girl killed with him, will again be plastered on the front page in bold print. Do you want to go through that again? Once you were only on the sidelines. This time you'd be right in the middle of it.'' He crossed the room and braced himself on the table, leaning over her. His face was only a few inches from hers. ''Are you prepared to go through all that litigation? Can you afford it financially? I've checked. With all the ambiguities of this case, no lawyer would touch it for less than five thousand dollars. Probably more. I promise you my parents will play to win. No expense or dirty tricks will be spared. They'll pull out all the stops. And what about Allison during that time? She'll probably become a ward of the state and be placed in a foster home until a decision is reached, which could be months. Is that what you want for her right now?''

Katherine clutched the baby to her and looked away from Jace. He was right! How could she fight against such odds? Even if she won in the long run, the price of victory would be too high. Then a new thought came to her.

"What if . . . just if . . . we went through with this marriage, wouldn't your parents fight us both?"

"They might fight me if I were trying to get guardianship of her by myself. Use the single-parent syndrome against me. But they wouldn't fight us both. Together we form a family unit. We would apply immediately for adoption. That would make her legally our child, not just our ward. Any court would favor that. And we're much younger than my parents, a strong point for our side. Besides that," he grinned sardonically, "I don't think they, particularly Mother, would like that kind of publicity." He chuckled softly. "As a matter of fact, as soon as they know we're married, they'll probably hold a press conference and declare how thrilled they are that their problem was resolved. They'll make it sound like it was all their idea and that they're thankful we found each other."

By this time Katherine had fed Allison, and the baby, whose innocent life was the source of so much conflict, had dropped off to sleep again. Katherine took her into the bedroom and placed her in the crib. Bath time would be postponed today.

When she returned to the kitchen, Jace was clearing up the dishes. "You'd better hurry and get dressed. We're supposed to meet the judge and Mark's friend at two o'clock."

"Jace, I can't marry you," she said reasonably. Maybe things weren't as bad as he was making them out to be. Anger was a wasted emotion now, but she resented his bullying her this way. "I can take care of Allison, and I can take care of myself."

Sparks of anger flashed in Jason's blue eyes as he turned toward her. His thumbs hooked into the belt loops of his jeans as he assumed a belligerent stance. "Well, forgive me for pointing out that you're doing a helluva job. Taking care of yourself, huh? Last night you almost got yourself raped by a horny old bastard who was coming on to you so strong that even *I* could pick up the vibes from him."

"That's not fair!" she cried. "I was a victim. Now you're victimizing me by coercing me into a marriage I want no part of."

He was furious now, taking slow, menacing steps to stand directly in front of her. He spoke with a deceptively serene voice. "Have you stopped to consider, Miss Adams, that I don't particularly want to sacrifice my freedom either? I didn't come halfway around the world, then halfway across the country to be married! Believe me, that was the furthest thing from my mind."

"Then why—"

"Because I feel responsible to provide that baby in there with a proper home. She's the real victim, Katherine. Not you or me. I'm willing to marry you in compensation for what Peter did to Mary. At the same time, you'll be keeping your promise to your sister." He stepped back a few feet and asked, "Now, are you ready to go with me to Dallas?"

She covered her face with her hands. Thinking was so difficult. Rational thought was impossible when he was so close. She could feel the angry heat emanating from his body. His breathing was labored. He was as agitated as she. There was no time to analyze her predicament. She had to decide now.

How could he remain so composed? Was he always so damned right? So logical? What were the choices? There were none. He knew it. She knew it.

"Okay, Jace." That was the only commitment she allowed him. It would have to do.

Silently she thanked him that there was no gloating in his manner when he said, "I'll be back in an hour. Do you want to stay in Dallas overnight or come back today?"

Overnight? With him? In a hotel room? "No. Why don't we just come back."

"Okay. Do you want to leave Allison with Happy?"

"No. If you don't mind, I'd rather take her. I don't want anyone to know about this until it's all over. Happy would want to—"

"I understand," he interrupted. "I'll see you in an hour then."

❧ ❧

The trip to Dallas was long and arduous. Jace had returned for them in precisely one hour, and Katherine had been frantic to get ready in time. She dressed in a soft yellow linen dress and wore a navy blue blazer over it. The ensemble was a far cry from a traditional wedding dress, but then, this was no traditional wedding.

Katherine was no longer surprised that Jace could wear anything and look magnificent in it. Today his navy blazer, camel slacks, cream shirt, and paisley tie would have made the models in *Gentleman's Quarterly* envious. He moved in dress clothes with the same alacrity and grace as he did when wearing jeans.

Jace suggested that they take her car to the city since the back seat of the jeep wasn't really safe enough for Allison to ride in even strapped into her car bed.

The drive from Van Buren to Dallas took only about two hours on the interstate highway, but those hours seemed like an eternity. Neither of them talked much. They were wary and careful of the other's deep thoughts, and therefore protected themselves with silence or small talk.

When they reached the suburbs, Jace stopped at a service station busy with Labor Day traffic and asked directions to the courthouse downtown.

Curiosity urged Katherine to ask, "How did you manage to obtain a marriage license?"

"I told you. Mark's friend will have it for us when we get there. All we'll have to do is sign it. And write in your middle name. I didn't know it." He took his eyes off the heavy traffic long enough to flash her a brilliant smile.

"June," she mumbled, still lost in the puzzle. "But aren't blood tests and things like that required?"

"A fraternity brother of mine is a doctor in Denver. He certified us both, and Mark sent the necessary papers here."

She was appalled. "That's illegal isn't it? Fraudulent?"

He only shrugged. "Maybe. I don't know." That mischievous glint she was learning to recognize was in his eyes as he asked conspiratorily, "Why? Do you think you might have syphilis?"

"Ohh," she ground through clenched teeth.

Jace laughed. "You'd better not get mad at me. Put on a blushing bride face, because we're here."

Finding a parking space on a holiday weekend was no problem and they stopped Katherine's small car directly in front of the historic red limestone building.

"Wait here a minute," Jace said as he eased himself from behind the wheel and walked toward two men who were standing on the steps of the deserted building. After a brief conference, Jace came back and said, "All set."

Katherine shook hands with both men, not caring to catch their names and trying not to meet their speculative eyes. They probably thought Allison was her baby and that this was a shotgun wedding. The license was signed with dispatch.

The wind was like a tornado as it whipped around the skyscrapers of downtown Dallas. Katherine struggled to keep her skirt down and still maintain a careful hold on Allison, who had begun to wail. Between vows, Jace took Allison from an abashed Katherine and cradled her against his shoulder. She quieted immediately.

It was over. Jace kissed Katherine perfunctorily on the lips when directed to, and they made their way back to the car. When Katherine and Allison were settled once more, he went back to the two men and, reaching into his pockets, took out a roll of bills. He paid each man, shook hands with them once more, and came back to the car.

Jace offered to stop somewhere to eat, but Katherine declined, longing for the sanctuary of her own house.

"Would you like to go to Neiman-Marcus and pick out a wedding present?" Jace asked as he maneuvered her car through the maze of downtown streets.

She was momentarily tempted, for she had never been in the famous store. Allison chose that moment to show her disapproval of the idea by starting to fret. Reluctantly, Katherine declined Jace's offer.

As usual, he was sensitive to her emotion and read her disappointment. "We'll come back sometime soon by ourselves. I promise."

The trip back to Van Buren was trying. The two adults were uptight and agitated with each other and their new status. Whether Allison sensed the tension between them or whether she was tired from the unconventional day and longing for her usual environs, she cried off and on all the way back.

Jace cursed the dimensions of the small car, declaring that the first thing he was going to do Tuesday morning was buy a decent one. "The biggest damn car I can find."

"Please watch your language in front of the baby," Katherine said sweetly.

He whipped his head toward her angrily and grazed his forehead on the sun visor. He cursed again, but this time under his breath.

By the time they reached the garage apartment, they were all hot, tired, hungry, and angry. Katherine fed Allison her supper of strained carrots and spinach which she sputtered all over herself and Katherine. That made the second bath of the day mandatory. It was with a great deal of relief that Katherine placed her in the crib for the night.

Katherine was exhausted and decided to take a bath herself. Jace, as soon as he had helped her carry Allison upstairs, left for his motel.

"I need to go pack my things and check out. It's been home for almost two weeks now. I'm sorry I don't have a home to offer you," he smiled. "Do you mind if we live in your apartment for a while?"

"No, of course not," she replied. Until that moment she hadn't thought past the wedding ceremony. Now the impact of what this marriage entailed hit her. She was going to be living with Jace. Living and what else? That question haunted her.

On trembling legs she left the bathroom and tiptoed

to her closet. She pulled on a University of Colorado T-shirt and her oldest, most faded pair of jeans. Then she slipped her feet into a pair of sandals. *Maybe if I don't look like a bride, I won't be expected to perform like one*, she thought hopefully. She brushed her hair and piled it on top of her head, securing it with combs.

Jace wasn't back yet when she started preparing dinner. He came whistling through the front door just as she was arranging cheese sandwiches on a hot grill.

"Do I have time for a shower?" he asked, poking his head around the corner.

"Yes, a quick one."

"Be right out. Baby okay?"

"Yes, she's down for the night."

"Good," he said and retreated into the back of the apartment toward the bathroom.

Good? Why was it good that Allison was down for the night? Did that get her out of the way? Katherine's hands trembled as she tore lettuce into a bowl.

To a can of mushroom soup, she added onions sauted in butter and two tablespoons of cooking sherry. Apparently Jace appreciated her efforts. After his first sip he cocked an eyebrow and said, "Not bad. You've passed your first test as a new wife."

Her first test? Were more to come? "I hope you like Swiss cheese on rye bread."

"Love it," he said with a wink. His hair was still damp from the shower, and he had dressed in jeans and a casual shirt. He hadn't secured all the buttons, and

Katherine noted that the thick mat of hair on his chest was damp and curled.

"If you don't mind, I'll wait until morning to unpack. I just dumped everything in the living room for now."

"N-no, that's . . . uh . . . fine," she stammered. Did all newlyweds find conversation this difficult?

When he raised a glass to his lips, she warned, "I don't sweeten my iced tea. If you—"

"I don't sweeten mine either. See how much we have in common already?" He took a long drink of the beverage and saluted her with the glass before setting it down. He was teasing her, but she was nervous and jumpy. He seemed so big. The small kitchen could barely contain him. His virility frightened her.

They ate in tense silence. As they finished, Katherine apologized for the simplicity of the meal. "I haven't gone to the grocery store in several days, and I had to make do with what I had."

"Don't apologize. It was delicious. I can look forward to the times when you want to impress me with your culinary talents. But don't think I expect you to cook all the time. I'm pretty handy in the kitchen too."

He smiled, the blue eyes twinkling. The dimples on the sides of his mouth deepened. Had she ever noticed the sensuous shape of his lips before now? Yes, she admitted, she had many times.

He was absently outlining the wood grain of the table top with his long, tapered finger. His hands were strong, yet gentle. The nails were trim and clean.

Katherine remembered how it had felt to have that hand stroking her breasts in the same way it now moved over the table top, slowly, soothingly, deliberately. That day at the lake, those same hands had raised her shirt and held her against his bare chest. When he kissed her, his fingers had fondled her nipples, tenderly squeezing them between—

Katherine jumped up from her chair, clattering the dishes as she bumped into the table. She couldn't sit here and look at him one moment longer. What insanity was this? One would think she had married him for romantic reasons. How absurd!

Jace reached across the table and grabbed her wrists with the precision of a striking snake. He stymied her impulse to pull away with a compelling stare. Imperiously he pulled her around the table toward him. He spread wide his knees and drew her between them, clasping her thighs with his own.

Releasing her wrists, he reached up and removed the combs from her hair. "I like your hair better down," he said softly as he watched it tumble to her shoulders. "It's an unusual color. Do you lighten it here?" He tugged playfully on a strand framing her face.

"No, it . . . the sun does that." Why was her throat so congested? She couldn't draw a deep breath.

"It's pretty," he murmured. His hands were firm on her back as he drew her closer. "You smell good." She could feel the moisture of his breath through her T-shirt.

"Come here, Katherine," he said gently and pulled her down onto his lap. He studied her face for a long time. "There's no reason for you to be acting like a skittish pony. I'm not going to force my husbandly rights on you. We won't share a bed until we've had time to get to know each other." He flashed her a wicked smile. "Even though I was encouraged last night."

Last night! Had it only been twenty-four hours since he rescued her from Ronald Welsh's assault? She flushed hotly remembering how she had welcomed his comfort, his passionate and intimate caresses, his kisses. During their fierce argument this morning, she had prayed he wouldn't use last night's behavior as a point of persuasion. He hadn't; he hadn't forgotten it either.

As these thoughts flickered through her mind, she looked at him in surprised wonder. Her expression must have conveyed a world of meaning, for he laughed.

"I haven't forced myself on a woman yet, and I don't intend to start with my wife. Besides, I haven't read the newspaper today."

He shoved her off his lap and gave her fanny a swat before he went into the living room. Katherine tried to bridle her capricious emotion. Irrationally, she was miffed that he could dismiss her so easily. Her body was burning with a desire generated by nothing more than his sheer masculinity. She was actually disappointed that he hadn't forced his conjugal rights on her!

"I think I'll go on to bed, Jace." She smiled tremulously as she came into the living room after cleaning up in the kitchen. "It's been a rather eventful day."

"Sure. Rest well."

"Good night then."

"Good night."

An hour later she was still tossing on the narrow bed when Jace opened the door to the bedroom. A fan of light arced across the bed as he stood silhouetted in the doorway.

"Mrs. Manning," he addressed her.

Her heart leaped to her throat and instinctively she pulled the sheet higher under her chin.

"Y-yes?" she stuttered.

"About that other bedroom—"

"Yes?"

"We have a problem."

"What?"

"There's no bed in it."

Katherine put her fingers over her lips to cover a laugh. "Oh, Jace. I didn't think! I'm sorry. When I moved in, I knew I would sleep in the same room with Allison until she was older. I bought this bed, but haven't—"

"Enough said," he sighed. "Well, I'd probably kick the slats out of the crib, and both of us would never fit on that," he indicated her day bed. "Or if we did, I could never uphold the terms of our agreement," he added huskily. He sighed a second time. "So, I guess it's the sofa for me."

Before he left he said, "A bed is right up there on the top of our shopping list along with a new car. I don't fit one damn thing in this whole damn house."

He slammed the door behind him, but Katherine knew it was out of exasperation and not anger.

She chuckled once again before turning over and falling into a restful sleep. Just on the brink of oblivion, she assured herself yet again that her responses to him the evening before had been out of gratitude. Her emotions had been highly charged and were running close to the surface. There was nothing else to it. She was positive of that, no matter what Jace wanted to read into it.

Chapter Six

✖✖

It was hard for Katherine to determine when she first began to lose her initial wariness of Jason Manning. For the first few days after their bizarre marriage ceremony, she was constantly on guard, weighing each word and rehearsing each gesture.

Jace didn't countenance her nervousness. He was scrupulously considerate, courteous, and helpful. He allowed her times to be alone, intuitively guessing correctly that she valued privacy.

Allison was a strong common bond between them. Watching Jace in the process of developing a relationship with his niece was delightful, and Katherine was relieved to know that his being a good parent wouldn't be a source of concern. Indeed, Allison sometimes preferred his company over hers.

"I think we'd better get dressed and go to church this morning," he said from behind the Sunday newspaper the morning after their marriage. He had come to the breakfast table painfully stretching the muscles that were cramped from sleeping on the sofa. Katherine laughed when she saw his grimace and heard his bones popping and cracking. For her display of levity, she received a quelling look.

"Church?" His suggestion surprised her.

"Yes. Happy's out in her backyard and has been for the past twenty minutes or so. She's done just about every odd job one can do in a backyard. She's glaring up at us in righteous indignation and censure. No doubt she's noted that my jeep was parked here overnight and probably thinks we're engaging in something illicit."

"Oh, I'd forgotten about that," Katherine anguished.

"We'll go down and make our announcement to her as soon as you're ready."

"Do you really want to go to church?"

"Yes. Unless we find our beliefs incompatible. I'm a Christian, a Protestant. Any problems there?"

"No, no, it's just that—"

"Katherine, have you thought about there being some gossip over the young Widow Adams suddenly marrying her long-lost brother-in-law? And the young Widow Adams having a baby only a few months old?

If the Mannings are going to live in Van Buren, I want it known right away that they are moral pillars of the community. I'll protect you any way I can from erroneous or slanderous speculation. We have absolutely nothing to hide except Allison's true parentage, and as soon as we can legally adopt her, that will no longer be an issue. And the best defense is a good offense.'' He looked at her from behind the newspaper and smiled. "Okay?"

"Thank you," she murmured. Tears were prickling her eyelids as she rushed out of the kitchen to take a bottle of milk to a demanding Allison. She didn't want to be obligated to him, but he made it necessary for her to be grateful. Didn't he ever overlook anything? Forget something?

Jace was happy to learn that some businesses were going to be open on Labor Day to take advantage of holiday shoppers. He bought a bed at one of the larger department stores and made arrangements for it to be delivered the following day.

"But, Jace, a king-size bed won't fit in that small room!" Katherine protested when she saw his choice.

"I'll make it fit to the exclusion of all other furniture. Any other size doesn't accommodate me." He laughed and squeezed her arm. "I promise not to mess up your decorating scheme too much."

He bought a new station wagon, and, much to Katherine's dismay, paid cash for it. Coming from a home where every penny had been stretched to its limit and budgeting was a way of life, Katherine couldn't conceive of someone having that much cash at one time.

The thought plagued her. She hadn't been cured of her aversion to the Mannings even though she was now married to one and bore that name herself. The thought that she was living on their money was repugnant. She broached the subject as they drove home from their shopping expedition.

"Jace—" she said timidly.

"Hmm?" He was snacking on a Hershey bar. She'd learned over the past few days that he had a constant craving for chocolate. Why didn't he get fat?

"You paid for Ronald Welsh's hospital bill, didn't you?"

He stopped his munching and glanced at her as he stopped the new car at a traffic light. "Yes," he said.

"And you sent some money to his wife?"

He answered with a nod.

She pleated the skirt of her sundress between her fingers as she continued hesitantly. "You have a lot of money. I mean, buying the car with cash and all. Is . . . your salary? I mean—"

"You're asking if the money is mine or my parents'." It wasn't a question. He had pulled the car to a stop in Happy's driveway and turned to look at her.

"The money is mine, Katherine." He showed a hint of a smile. "And I came by it honestly by working my buns off. When I left Africa, I was due a large bonus.

Willoughby Newton, the owner of Sunglow, is very fair. I have a share in every well I bring in. Since I left for college, I've not taken a penny from my parents.''

"I didn't mean to pry into your private affairs. I just didn't—''

"You didn't want to live on any money from Eleanor and Peter Manning, Sr., because you have a lot of pride." His voice lowered in volume and pitch as he said, "I have a lot of pride in you." He edged across the seat toward her and tilted her chin up with his finger, forcing her to look at him. "And my private affairs are your affairs now. You're my wife, remember?''

His lips caressed hers softly and gently. It was a brief kiss, passionless, but Katherine could feel the constrained desire behind it. Her heart thumped wildly when he pulled back and looked at her with his fathomless blue eyes. She was drowning in them before he moved away and got out of the car.

Happy took the news of their marriage with immediate joyful acceptance. If she speculated on a former relationship or the brevity of their courtship, she kept her conjectures to herself. For that Katherine was grateful.

Happy offered to watch Allison for the rest of the afternoon while they painted a wall in Jace's bedroom. Katherine insisted that they do it before the bed was delivered the next day.

"With the two of us painting, it won't take long, I promise," she said when her suggestion was met with grumbles.

"Who ever heard of laboring on Labor Day?" Jace asked, but approached the project enthusiastically when Katherine changed into the painting costume she had been wearing the first time he saw her.

"You look great in that get-up, you know," Jace said as they took a break from their efforts. She was sitting Indian fashion on the floor, sipping a soft drink. "Just don't ever let me catch you answering the door in it again," he threatened with a growl.

He stared at her through slitted lids and said softly, "The first time I saw your legs, it took all of my self-control not to accost you right then."

"What?" She was startled by this revelation. "When?"

"Uhh, let's see." He closed one black-fringed eye in concentration. "I think it was the second day after I got to town. I went to the campus and stalked the halls of your office building. I was curious and wanted to catch a glimpse of the elusive Miss Katherine Adams who so daringly took a premature newborn out of the hospital and drove across the country with her."

He sipped the soft drink and leaned back against the wall. "You came out of your office and walked to the water fountain. I think you took a couple of aspirin. Anyway, when you leaned over to get a drink, I had a very advantageous view of your legs . . . and other things." His eyes were twinkling with devilry.

Embarrassment closed Katherine's throat for a few

moments before she said tartly, "But that couldn't be true! I'd have seen you in the hall. I'm sure I would have noticed you."

He raised an eyebrow, as his interest was piqued. His voice was low when he said, "Oh, yeah?" He scooted across the floor on his bottom, propelling himself with strong arms. "Does that mean, Mrs. Manning, that you find your husband to be somewhat attractive?"

"It . . . I mean . . . you—"

"Yes?" he asked softly as his hands settled on her shoulders. Gently, but firmly, he lowered her to the floor. "What were you about to say?" His face was less than an inch from hers. He stretched out full length beside her, and she felt the weight of his body pressing close.

"I was about to say—"

"It can wait," he barely managed to whisper before his mouth descended on hers.

Katherine eagerly welcomed his kiss. She knew what a delicious, tingling warmth it could spread through her body. She opened her mouth under the unhurried, seeking lips. Shyly she touched the tip of her tongue to his. A low groan issued from deep in his throat as his mouth became more urgent. His hand stroked the bare skin of her midriff.

He placed one knee on the inside of her thighs and applied sweet, but earnest, pressure. He, too, was wearing shorts, and the touch of his skin on hers was an electrifying sensation. Tantalizingly, he rubbed his leg along hers. The hairs on his long thigh prickled her smooth skin. How different were the smell and feel and texture of his body in contrast to hers. The differences ignited her with a longing to know them better.

He buried his face in her neck, murmuring unintelligible words, planting ardent kisses on her warm flesh as he groped for the buttons of her shirt. "Katherine, Katherine, I want—"

"Hey, you two, I made some sandwiches for you. You must be getting hungry. Come open the door. My hands are full." Happy's voice came to them from the front door.

"I can't believe it!" Jace smacked his forehead with his palm as he stood and stalked into the living room to let the overzealous landlady in.

※ ※

"That's the second time Happy has interrupted an intimate moment. Am I going to have to tie a necktie on the doorknob like Ryan O'Neal did in *Love Story* each time he had Ali McGraw in his room?"

"Jace, please!" Katherine acted indignant, but she giggled.

Happy had come and gone quickly. She wouldn't leave Allison unattended for more than a minute. Katherine and Jace ate the sandwiches and returned to their work. The painting was finished and now they were clearing away the mess.

"I like the room this way," Jace commented. "I thought the brown wall would make it too dark."

"Not with all the windows on the south side." Katherine had given the room's decor careful consideration. She hadn't thought that it would ever be occupied by a man and had immediately made some adjustments in her original plans.

The bed would go against the toast brown wall. Today on their shopping spree she purchased linens with a shell motif in browns and beiges. The only feminine touch she allowed was accents in a soft apricot.

"Eventually, I'd like to get a brass headboard. I think it would look super against that dark wall. Then I'll use brass for decorating too. Lamps, things like that." She was envisioning her finished project even as she mused aloud. "Of course, it might get crowded in here. I'll have to see how much floor space that bed is going to take up."

"I hope it'll get even more crowded in here—soon."

Jace's tone of voice catapulted her out of her musings and she looked at him suspiciously. He stared at her from under hooded eyes, but the light radiating from them made his implication clear.

She was flustered, but refused to show it and tossed her head indifferently. He saw through her ruse and grinned broadly. "I'll run down and get Allison. I think the paint fumes have cleared out enough."

He went toward the door, but turned back to her. "Katherine."

"Hmm?"

"I really *was* in your office building one day, and I *did* see you walking down the hall." He winked. "I only fantasized the rest."

She blushed to the roots of her hair. But he didn't see it. He was already gone.

"Hi, Miz Manning, I'm Jim Cooper."

Katherine smiled at the friendly young man who stood at her front door, but was puzzled at his reason for being there. He seemed to expect her to recognize him.

She shook her head slightly and said, "I'm sorry—"

"I'm Happy Cooper's son."

"Oh." Katherine laughed. "Come in. I'm sorry. For a minute the name didn't do anything for me." She extended her hand and Jim Cooper shook it heartily.

"I guess Mom forgot to tell you that I was moving back for a while. Not here," he clarified. "Another guy and I are sharing an apartment across town. I ran up to see if Mr. Manning was home."

"No, I'm sorry, he's not. He went out to do some shopping for himself. He only moved in a few days . . . I mean . . . we haven't . . ."

"Yeah. Mom told me you were newlyweds." His grin was engaging. "Best wishes."

"Thank you," Katherine mumbled. She was unaccustomed to thinking of herself as a married woman, being addressed as Mrs. Manning. She wondered if she would ever get used to bearing that name. And it seemed strange having to account for someone else. Only a week ago she had herself and Allison to care about. Now her life included the very dynamic presence of Jace Manning. His whereabouts, habits, and personality were becoming entwined with hers.

"While I'm here Mom strongly suggested I check the attic. Some of my stuff from high school and college is up there, and you could probably use the extra storage space." Jim Cooper grinned again, and Katherine noticed his good looks for the first time. Was he already out of college? He must be older than she had thought him to be.

His sandy hair was longer than current styles dictated, but it was trimmed and clean. His eyes were a warm brown and bespoke his open, friendly manner. A sprinkling of freckles across his cheeks and nose contributed to his boyish and mischievous appearance.

"I haven't even looked in the attic," Katherine admitted. "Don't feel you have to move anything for us."

"I'll just scout it out today. This was Mom's idea. Even if I find some memorabilia from my school days, I think I can live without it." He stood at attention with his hand over his heart, and Katherine laughed.

He seemed so short compared to Jace, she thought absently, then chided herself for the comparison. Why had Jace suddenly become the standard by which she judged every other man?

Objectively, Jim wasn't as tall, but showed no inclinations toward obesity like his mother. His ragged cutoffs showed off well-proportioned legs, and a white T-shirt snugly fit his muscled torso.

"The door to the attic is in here, isn't it, Miz Manning?" he asked as he made his way toward the bedroom in which Jace slept.

"Yes," Katherine answered as she followed him. "In the closet. And I'm Katherine."

Jim preceded her, and, when she went into the room, he was already in the closet lowering the ladder which disappeared into the attic. With youthful agility, he climbed the steps and switched on the light in the small space above.

Katherine heard him thumping around among the boxes, exclaiming when some forgotten treasure was uncovered. She stood at the bottom of the ladder, looking up into the square of light.

"Are you finding some golden goodies?" she asked teasingly.

"You bet! I'd forgotten about most of this sh—uh . . . stuff. Maybe I'll take down some of the boxes."

He began carrying them down the ladder one by one and stacking them in the middle of the bedroom floor. He made several trips before he said, "Just one more, and I'll get out of your way."

"No hurry," Katherine assured him. "Allison's asleep, and I'm free until she wakes up."

"Yeah. I heard you had a real little doll there. I can't

wait to meet her," Jim said over his shoulder as he ascended the stairs for the last box.

He scooted the box close to the opening for easier access. Katherine was looking up at him when she was showered with grit and dust dislodged by the sliding box. A particle fell into her eye and she cried out in pain.

"Oh!" she exclaimed, putting a hand over her eye.

"What's wrong?" Jim asked. Alarmed, he bounded down the ladder. "Oh, gosh, what happened?" He hovered over her anxiously. "Mom'll have my ass for sure if I did something to hurt you."

Only the searing pain in her eye prevented Katherine from laughing. "It's my eye. Something fell into it." She winced at the stinging sensation and pressed her eye more firmly with her hand.

"Oh, God, I'm sorry. Here, Katherine, sit down." Solicitously, Jim took her arm and led her toward the bed. Blindly, she sat down and Jim braced himself on the bed with one knee. "Here, Katherine," he said gently, "let me see."

He tried to take her hand away from the offended eye. She submitted, then as the grit found a new spot to irritate, she jerked her hand back.

"Ouch! It hurts if I take my hand away."

"I know, but you've got to let me get that crud out of there or your eye may really get hurt. Come on now," he persisted as he removed her hand.

"Now open your eye," he instructed.

He cupped her head in one of his hands while with the other he worked with utmost care on her eye. It took some coaxing from him to get her to open her eye for his examination.

He shouted triumphantly when he spotted the tiny grain of sand that was causing her so much discomfort. "Here we go," Jim said confidently. "Look up now. No, no, don't look down. Look up. One more second. There now. There!" His deft finger had managed to lift the particle from her eye.

"I hope I'm not interrupting anything," Jace said.

Chapter Seven

✿ ✿

The deadly voice was like a cannon shot in the room. Katherine turned quickly with blurred, watering eyes to see Jace leaning negligently against the door jamb. His stance was deceptive. His rigid jaw and frigid eyes were clues to his extreme displeasure.

"Let me put it another way," he continued when the two shocked people on the bed failed to move or speak. "I'd better *not* be interrupting anything." He fixed a cold, blue stare on Jim Cooper.

Nervously, Katherine rose to her feet. She hadn't realized that she was lying on the bed supported by her elbows. Jim was leaning over her, cradling her head with one hand. His face was inches from hers.

"J-Jace," she stammered and cursed herself for being self-conscious. "This is Jim Cooper, Happy's son."

"Mr. Manning," Jim nodded and smiled tentatively. He swallowed hard when Jace didn't respond to the introduction.

"Jim came over to get some things out of the attic. Some sand fell in my eye while I was looking up. He helped me get it out." Katherine despised herself for explaining the incident to him. She hadn't done anything unseemly and neither had poor Jim. The features of Jace's face didn't soften. He didn't even blink to relieve that glacial stare.

"Mr. Manning, I wanted to see you about something else," Jim said haltingly. Katherine commended him for his courage. Jace, in spite of his relaxed pose, presented a formidable mien.

"Yes?" he asked shortly.

"I was going to ask about a job with Sunglow. I . . . uh . . . I've been working for an independent drilling company in Louisiana, but my mom, being alone and all, well, I . . . uh . . . thought I might . . . ought to . . ."

Jace shifted his weight from one foot to the other and folded his arms across his chest in boredom. Katherine seethed in anger at his superior attitude over the young man.

When Jim saw Jace's impatience, he hurried on.

"Anyway, I need a job. I'm a good roughneck. I have letters of recommendation." He licked his dry lips when he finished.

Jace flicked his eyes in Katherine's direction then leveled them on Jim Cooper once again. She was gratified to see that Jim met Jace's stare undauntedly.

"You've got the nerve to ask me about a job after I just caught you on a bed with my wife?" Jace sounded condescendingly amused.

"Jace, I—" Katherine's words died in her throat when he shot her a quelling look.

"But I like your mother," Jace went on, as if she hadn't spoken. "See Billy Jenkins. Do you know where we're drilling?"

"Yes, sir," Jim answered.

"All right. Tell Billy I sent you.'

"Thank you, Mr. Manning." Jim indicated the boxes on the floor. "I'll take this one now," he said lifting up the smallest of them, "and come back later for the rest. If that's okay," he added quickly.

"That's fine, Jim." Katherine smiled.

"Well, I'll be going then. Bye, Kath . . . uh . . . Miz Manning," he amended, looking nervously at Jace.

He tried to ease himself past Jace, who still blocked the doorway, but Jace gripped him on the shoulder and held him fast. "If you screw up out there, you're out. No matter whose son you are."

"Yes, sir. I understand," Jim averred solemnly.

Jace released him and nodded in acknowledgment.

Katherine and Jace stared at each other until they heard the front door slam. Katherine was furious with her new husband. His attitude was inexcusable. The high and mighty Mannings.

Her eyes were flashing green fire when she flared, "How dare you treat someone—anyone—so abominably in my house."

"He's lucky I didn't break his neck. I don't particularly like the idea of coming home and finding my wife in a clinch with another man."

"I just met him minutes before you walked in!" she defended. "He came here to see you and carry out his mother's instructions. You intentionally humiliated him. He's just a boy."

Jace laughed bitterly. "Oh, sure. A twenty-two-year-old boy. Believe me, Katherine, Mr. Cooper was enjoying holding you in his arms no matter for what urgent reason. Any healthy, red-blooded man would."

"Don't judge everyone else by your own animalistic standards," she snapped.

"Have you forgotten Mr. Welsh?" Jace asked with an eyebrow cocked in mockery.

"Oh!" she sputtered. "You're nothing but a big bully."

Livid with anger, she flew across the room. She raised her small hand and slapped him as hard as she could on his firm jaw.

The breath whooshed out of her body as he grasped her around the waist with one steel arm and yanked her against him. His fist tangled in her hair, and he pulled her head back painfully so she was forced to look at him.

Her fear was championed only by her disbelief. She had slapped him! His temper was nothing to take lightly. It had erupted on the day they went to the lake. It was unleashed again, even more violently, on Ronald Welsh. Now his eyes bored into her, and she held her breath in shrinking apprehension.

To her absolute surprise, he burst out laughing.

"You're quite a little wildcat when pushed too far, aren't you, Katherine?" His face moved to within inches of hers, and she could feel his breath on her hot cheeks. "And you're gorgeous," he rasped. "When you're mad, you're exquisite."

His lips crushed hers even as his embrace became more binding. She was still angry and tried vainly to push him away. But her thrusting hands against the wall of his chest were ineffectual, and she gave up her efforts about the same time his tongue insinuated its way into her mouth.

The hands which had strained against him were now weaving through the luxuriant richness of his hair. His hand moved to the side of her face, and he stroked her cheek with his thumb while his mouth demanded more . . . and more.

At last he drew away. He continued to look down at her tenderly as his index finger smoothed over her stubble-chafed, burning lips. "Katherine, I knew why young Cooper was up here. I saw his mother outside before I came in. But don't disillusion yourself. I'm fiercely possessive.'' He kissed her lightly on the nose before he turned and left the room.

His volatile moods confused her, bewildered her. Would she ever know the person, Jason Manning, completely?

※ ※

The president of Van Buren College had given Katherine the following week off. When Jace had called him about Ronald Welsh, the administrator had asked him to convey that message to her.

''He said there had been five or six girls over a period of about two years in that office. Now they know why,'' he said disdainfully. ''Anyway, they're sending over a new guy from the administration building to revamp the whole public relations department. He said you wouldn't be needed this week, but, of course, you'll be paid.'' His contempt was plain. ''Do you want to go back?''

''I don't know,'' Katherine answered honestly. ''So much has happened these past few days, I really haven't given it much thought. I don't think I could sit idle here in the apartment with only Allison to look after. I've worked ever since I was in high school.''

''Well, think about it this week,'' Jace suggested logically. ''Something unexpected might turn up.'' His smile was enigmatic, but no amount of persuasion on her part would coax him to elaborate.

Katherine thought back to this conversation as she stepped out of the shower and slipped into a lightweight wrapper. What was behind the mysterious words Jace had spoken to her last night? What was he planning now? Why wouldn't he tell her?

Jace could be extremely stubborn at times. Each day she saw a new facet of his personality. Grudgingly she admitted that most of them were favorable.

She finished applying her makeup and drying her hair. Straightening up the dressing table, she noted the masculine objects which had suddenly invaded her feminine domain.

She picked up Jace's injector razor. His initials were engraved in the sterling silver handle. Who had given it to him? It wasn't the kind of thing one bought for oneself. A woman? He had never mentioned previous affairs, though Katherine was certain there must have been many.

What was the middle initial L for? She didn't even know her husband's full name. Hadn't he asked for hers just before they were married? She couldn't remember. That day was like a hazy dream in her brain.

A matching sterling cup held his spicy shaving soap. Didn't most men use an aerosol foam? She was so ignorant of the opposite sex.

Every once in a while Katherine had a foggy memory of her father. She could recall special things he'd said or done. Once he'd punished her, then wept louder than she had after the spanking. That was a vivid recollection.

But she couldn't remember his things. All of his possessions had seemed to vanish from their house when he vanished from their lives. Had he used such a razor?

A bottle of masculine fragrance caught her eye and she reached for it. She studied the label and recognized the name. The television commercials touting this particular product were very suggestive.

"Nothing comes between my woman and me except my Temper."

The handsome male model was always shirtless and lying in bed with a sheet discreetly covering him from the hips down. Another time he rode into the camera on a motorcycle and showered gravel in all directions before the camera came in for a close-up. He said, "My Temper doesn't always show, but it's there."

Katherine noticed all commercials, for she aspired to write them. She smiled at the Temper ads. Weren't they just a bit trite? She held the bottle of cologne to her nose and sniffed it with absentminded appreciation.

Or were the men on Madison Avenue right on the pulse of things? Wasn't her heart beating faster after catching one fragrant whiff? Strange. It wasn't the model's face her mind conjured up. It was—

Katherine jumped in surprise and guilty abashment as the door opened behind her.

Jace looked at her in the mirror and said teasingly, "I hope you like it."

Katherine thought with a detached part of her mind that the model who represented Temper had nothing over the man who was her husband.

"Yes, yes, I do. I was just . . . uh . . ." Why was she stammering like a blithering idiot? This was her house first!

"Allison's down for her nap. I was reading the newspaper to her, but she konked out after the front page." He grinned.

"Thank you for watching her. It's nice being able to take a leisurely bath without having to listen for her."

"You're welcome. My small contribution was well worth the results. You look beautiful this morning." He came forward and turned her to face him. Their conversation had been conducted in the mirror. He enfolded her in his arms, but only brushed a kiss on her forehead.

"I've got to go out to the drilling site today, so I may not be back until late this evening." He was dressed for work in a very old, very tight pair of faded jeans, an equally faded short-sleeved shirt, and scuffed cowboy boots.

"Are they drilling yet?"

"If they did everything they were supposed to do last week, they should be able to start today. Incidentally, your friend Jim Cooper has joined the ranks."

She looked up at him. He hadn't released her from his arms. "You're the foreman, aren't you?" Having spent this short time in his company she sensed that he had downplayed his position with the oil company. Sunglow was one of the most prestigious oil companies in America, and holding even a junior executive's job would be no small feat.

"Yeah, in a manner of speaking," he shrugged. "But I couldn't do without my crew. They're all good men. We've been together a long time."

His shrugging motion had caused a tremor to course through Katherine's body. By his holding her tightly, she was made acutely aware of his least movement. When his chest stirred against her breasts, she involuntarily responded with a physical reaction.

His perception didn't fail him. He recognized the change in her instantly. "Are they still bothering you?" he asked kindly. "The scratches and bruises on your breasts? We may have to take you to a doctor yet." He sounded genuinely worried.

"No, Jace," she rushed to assure him. "They're healed and I'm fine."

"Let me see."

"What?" The soft question exploded out of her mouth in a puff of air. "No, really, it's . . . they're . . ."

Her voice trailed off as he stepped away from her and deftly untied the sash of her wrapper. Slowly, his hands parted the garment. She held her breath as his gaze took in the length of her naked body before his eyes came to rest on her breasts.

The angry red scratches left by Ronald Welsh's assault had faded to thin pink lines. The bruises were now only faint shadows on the honey-toned skin.

"I . . . I think you're right. They're healing okay." Jace's voice was strangled and hoarse. He lifted his eyes to hers. She read in them apology and supplication as his arm went inside the robe and encircled her waist. With his other hand he cupped a breast. His touch was so gentle she wasn't sure she didn't imagine it.

The dark head bent toward her and Katherine closed her eyes and parted her lips to receive his kiss. He moved his lips over hers and drew her closer until her sensitive skin knew intimately the soft fabric of his clothes. His mouth was possessive but gave as much as it took, delighting her with the slightest flicking of his tongue.

He ventured to her neck and nuzzled the hollow of her throat with his mouth. Ever so lightly his thumb brushed across her nipple. Like a bow string being pulled taut, Katherine arched her back. A small moan escaped her.

His mouth hovered over her breast. Katherine felt his warm breath on her skin as his thumb continued its lazy stimulation, arousing her to inconceivable passion.

When her nipple was a peak of desire begging for assuagement, she pleaded, "Jace—"

He groaned against her, "Oh, God, sweetheart." Then his mouth captured the aching nipple and surrounded it with a sweet, wet warmth.

The raven black hair tickled her skin as his head pressed against her chest. Katherine caught his head with impatient hands and held it fast, lest his mouth cease the delicious, gentle pull. His hand slid lower on her hip, pressing her nearer and demanding her to realize the strength of his desire. Without even being aware of her motion, Katherine rotated her hips against that thrilling force in a rhythmic massage.

His breath was ragged as he pushed her away from him with a swift shove. He hung his head for a moment, gulping in long breaths while he maintained a strong grip on her upper arms.

Katherine trembled in anxiety. Once when she had allowed a date to indulge in what she considered to be harmless necking, he had become aroused to the point of no return. He was furious when she denied him appeasement and had slapped her, calling her ugly names and accusing her of deliberately leading him on. Though he had crudely satisfied himself with his hand and disgusted her with apologies and excuses afterward, she knew his aspersions had been largely the truth. She liked the kissing and stroking but had never cared enough for anyone to complete the act. In sexual games she hadn't played fair, and she knew it. For some reason she didn't want Jace to think she was tormenting him with some diabolical trick in mind.

"Jace?" she asked tremulously. "Are you all right?" His face was flushed and his shoulders still heaved while he inhaled harshly.

He laughed ruefully. "Hardly," he said. "But if you keep on doing things like that, I'll never leave today, and I really need to go to work."

She had returned his passion. She confessed to that. If he had wanted to consummate their marriage, she would have been eager to participate.

"I'm sorry," she said and meant it. She felt the loss, the dissatisfaction, as surely as he did.

"Sorry?" His blue eyes sparkled. "I'm not one bit sorry that my wife has the body of a goddess." He planted a smacking kiss between her breasts before he closed her robe and tied the sash with regretful finality. "You've probably made it damned hard for me to keep my mind on my business today, but I'll make such a sacrifice any day." He sighed theatrically and chucked her under the chin before he left.

Chapter Eight

The following Saturday morning Jace asked Katherine if she wanted to drive out to the drilling site with him.

"I've put the crew on overtime. I'd like to run out there and check on things. It shouldn't take long. Would you like to go?"

The past week had been a welcomed relief from Katherine's normal early morning routine. Getting Allison bathed, dressed, fed, and carried to Happy's house before leaving for work was a dreaded task. Katherine had enjoyed these unexpected mornings off.

She managed to keep busy, rearranging closets and drawers, making room for the new resident in her house.

Toward the end of the week she ran out of projects and was growing restless. Having worked most of her life, idleness was far more tiring to her than labor.

"Yes, I'd like that," she said in response to Jace's invitation. "I've never been near an oil derrick before." Listening to him talk about his work had broadened her vocabulary.

"Well, I've been getting a lot of flack from the crew," he complained. "They think you're a figment of my imagination. They're not going to believe that I do indeed have a wife and baby daughter until I present you to them. Of course, Jim Cooper has been singing your praises to the sky, but no one puts much stock in that besotted kid."

She glanced at him in irritation, but it pleased her to know that he had mentioned her to the men he worked with. Why it pleased her, she didn't stop to examine. A warm sensation surrounded her heart as she looked at him across the breakfast table—a breakfast he had insisted on cooking.

She asked with feigned nonchalance, "What did you tell them about me?"

"Let's see. If I recall"—he drawled and squinted his eyes in deep concentration—"I told them that you had hair the color of honey with sunlight shining through it. Your eyes, I described as deep forest pools with overhead trees reflected in them. I told them that your body was beyond description, except to say that your bosom was of unbelievable proportions. Of course, you never wear any underwear even under the tight T-shirts and supertight jeans you prefer.''

''Jace! You couldn't—'' she cried before she caught the mischievous glint in his eyes. When he burst out laughing at her chagrin, she couldn't help but join in. Allison gazed at them both in bored condescension.

''I'm afraid if that's how you described me, they'll be sorely disappointed.''

His black brows hooded his eyes as he said softly, ''No. They won't be disappointed.''

Her heart did a somersault. Not since the morning when he had kissed her in the bathroom had he made any overt advances. She knew by now that aggression wasn't his style. He conquered with subtlety. All week his kisses had amounted to no more than affectionate pecks on the cheek or forehead. She found it disconcerting that somehow his restraint made her long for his touch.

One evening he had asked her to join him on the sofa to watch the late news on television. She settled herself at the opposite end of the sofa, but he said, ''Un-uh,'' and drew her closer to him. He was leaning back comfortably in the other corner, propped up on cushions.

She tucked bare feet under her light robe and in minutes realized that she had allowed herself to relax against him. She felt his steady breathing as his hard chest supported her back.

She started when he began stroking her upper arm with the hand that had been resting on the back of the sofa. She glanced at him quickly, but he was seemingly preoccupied with the newscast.

His motion was slow and hypnotic, tickling the inside of her arm with sensuous strokes. The strong tapering fingers imperceptibly moved closer to her breast. She could feel their movements on the soft curve without his actually touching it. The fabric of her robe stirred against his knuckles, so close was he to touching her. But he did not.

Her nipple became erect with longing and there was a heavy warmth in the lower part of her body. By the end of the broadcast, she was tempted to capture his hand and press it to her. His fingers finally stilled and Katherine held her breath. *Now he'll touch me*, she thought.

To her intense disappointment he patted her arm in a filial fashion and eased her up. "I guess I'd better get to bed," he said.

That night her body had tingled with unsatisfied sensations as she tossed restlessly on her narrow bed. Had he invited her onto the new king-size bed, she would have accepted gladly. Was this then his particular form of cruelty?

Peter had charmed Mary into loving him and then tortured her with physical and verbal abuse. Was Jace's method different only in that he tortured with a silken touch? Was he planning to make her care for him, only to torment her with rejection?

She resolved not to care. Falling in love with Jace

Manning would be a slow kind of death, for she knew that he didn't love her. He wanted her physically. His constraint hadn't dissolved his desire. It was evident in his kindling blue eyes that she often caught staring at her.

But his reasons for marrying her had been explicitly enumerated. He was compensating for Peter's treatment of Mary. He was fulfilling a responsibility he felt for Allison. He had even said that he didn't want to get married, and, that by doing so, he was sacrificing his freedom.

As Jace had predicted, his lawyer friend, Mark, sent them a newspaper clipping announcing their marriage. With uncanny clairvoyance Jace had been correct about his parents' reversal. The article quoted them as saying that Jace and Katherine had developed a deep attachment soon after they met (when was that to have been?), and, as Jace's parents, they were thrilled that he had married sweet Mary's sister.

Katherine had been furious when she read it. Jace only shrugged and tossed the clipping in the wastepaper basket. Maybe he wasn't as contemptuous of his parents as he pretended. Did he have an affinity for them that he concealed when it was expedient to do so? Like when convincing someone it would be to her advantage to marry him?

Now, as Katherine looked at his beguiling smile across the table, she warned herself again to be careful with her emotions.

"I'll get Allison dressed, and we can go whenever you like," she said.

❧ ❧

They drove through the east Texas countryside for about half an hour. Katherine enjoyed the scenery. The woods were thick with pine, cedar, native oaks, and elm. Now and then she glimpsed the graceful dogwood. In the spring it, with its glorious white or pink blossoms, would shame the towering giants that dwarfed it.

The country road narrowed and dwindled to little more than a pothole-ridden trail. The jeep bounced over the road, jarring their teeth and preventing conversation. Katherine clutched Allison to her, fearful that the baby would fly out of her arms when they hit a large bump.

Jace turned off the road and struck out across the pine-tree-dotted field that was somewhat more level. As they came to a clearing, the drilling rig came into view. Katherine was amazed by the activity and noise. The equipment required for the project was awesome.

Several of the crew stopped their work for a moment to wave to Jace as he bounded out of the jeep. He directed Katherine to stay put. He jogged to a disreputable-looking trailer whose peeling, faded gray paint was its most redeeming feature. Moments later Jace emerged wearing a hard hat and carrying another.

He shouted over the noise, "Here, put this on."

Katherine looked at the bright yellow helmet skeptically.

"Sorry. Mr. Manning's rules." He winked at her and plopped the hard hat on her head. He took Allison in his arms and carried her toward the trailer.

Katherine self-consciously climbed out of the jeep carrying her purse and Allison's diaper bag. She could feel the furtive glances directed toward her, though the roughnecks continued working with deliberation. She didn't try to distinguish Jim Cooper. The workmen had taken on the anonymity of an army. Were her jeans too tight, she wondered in panic, remembering what Jace had told her earlier.

The hard hat seemed like a ridiculously unnecessary precaution, but Jace had often referred to the strict rules he enforced at any site he worked on.

"Back in the thirties during the big boom in Texas men needed jobs desperately. They found work in the oil fields whether they were qualified or not. The wildcatters who hired them for peanuts didn't care about the danger involved. They were only glad to have a supply of cheap labor.

"It wasn't until later that safety regulations were put into effect. Unfortunately, many men were killed or seriously injured in unnecessary accidents. There's always the risk of having an accident around any derrick, but I try to lower the odds of one happening by enforcing as many safety precautions as possible." Apparently even his wife wasn't exempt.

Jace now stood on the steps of the trailer and held the door for Katherine. When she glanced up at him, he smiled broadly. *One would actually think he was proud of me*, she thought.

"Katherine, meet Billy Jenkins. He's mean and grouchy, bullheaded, coarse, and totally without scruples, but we're used to him."

Katherine took off the hard hat and looked at the man Jace had introduced to her in that unorthodox way. Billy was older than the other men. She wondered if Jace had assigned him duties in the trailer in deference to his age.

Billy's sparse hair was gray and frizzy. His complexion was like a piece of dry, brown leather stretched over his facial bones. Deep lines etched his face like a roadmap. Bowed legs and a stocky torso made him appear even shorter in stature than he was.

He looked Katherine up and down several times. His perusal wasn't lewd, just appreciative. "I want to know how a sweet, pretty little thing like you got hitched up with a goddamn slant-holer like him." He indicated Jace with an impertinent jerk of his small, round head.

The insult referred to someone who drilled diagonally into another well. During the boom, this was a heinous crime, and the culprit was considered to be the lowest of creatures.

From behind her Katherine heard Jace's deep, rumbling chuckle. "Are you just going to stand there insulting me, or are you going to get us something to drink?"

"Get it your own self. I want to see the baby."

Katherine knew the source of their bantering was a mutual affection. Billy stepped up to Jace and took Allison out of his arms. The baby immediately reached for the red handkerchief in Billy's shirt pocket and the old man laughed gleefully.

"That's a girl. You know who your friends are, don't you? You stick with old Billy, and you'll have fun. Yes, you will. Let's go over here and see something pretty." Billy carried the mesmerized Allison to his littered desk, speaking to her in dulcet tones.

Katherine and Jace laughed. "Nothing will make a fool out of someone as quickly as a baby," Jace said. He looked down at Katherine and winked. "Except maybe a beautiful woman. I thought I might be forced to defend your honor when Billy got a good look at you."

"I was flattered," she smiled. "I think he's a perfect gentleman," she said primly.

"What! That old reprobate? You glare at me every time I use language like he just did."

"Yes, but that's different."

"Why?"

"Because I'm not married to him. I'm married to you."

He looked at her sternly, though the corners of his mouth twitched with suppressed mirth. "That's right and don't you ever forget it," he growled.

They both laughed, and, impulsively, he reached out

and hugged her close. Katherine was still breathless from the quick, tight embrace when he opened a rusted refrigerator and took out two cold drinks. Allison was happy sitting in Billy's lap and basking in his ardent attention.

"Come over here," Jace said. "I want to make you a proposition." He gestured to a desk at the end of the trailer.

She followed him through the narrow confines, and he offered her the chair behind the desk. By comparison, it made Billy's desk look neat. It was covered with charts, maps, and diagrams. She could only guess at what they represented, but was curious as to the proposition he had mentioned.

He reached over her shoulder and picked up a sheet of paper. Katherine supposed that some sort of message could be deciphered from the bold, slanted scrawl. "I got this memo from Willoughby. He's the owner of Sunglow. I've referred to him." At her nod, he went on.

"It seems that Willoughby is concerned about the current reputation of the oil companies. Windfall profits and all that. He's resolved to do something about Sunglow's public image. He managed to swing a deal with several television stations in the larger markets of Texas and Oklahoma—Houston, Dallas, Fort Worth, Austin, Oklahoma City among others. Sunglow will provide maintenance service and gasoline for all their news cars, mobile units, and the like in exchange for commercial time.''

He took a drink of his soda and asked, "Are you following? Feel free to interrupt. It took me a while to digest it."

"Yes, I follow you, but—"

"Here comes the part that involves you. He needs someone to write the commercials. I recommended you."

Katherine stared up at him stunned. "Me!" she shrieked. "Jace, I don't know anything about—"

"Oil? You don't have to. What Willoughby wants is public-service-type commercials taken from the consumer's point of view. He wants to put forth the idea that Sunglow is concerned about the energy situation and is taking steps to rectify it and at the same time keep a tight rein on the price of gasoline. We need our reputation improved. You've had experience in public relations. You've written press releases. This'll be a snap."

"Is Sunglow really doing that though? I couldn't lie."

He looked almost pained before saying, "Katherine, I wouldn't ask you to lie. Do you think I'd be affiliated with a company that was fleecing the public?"

She looked away from him. "No." She gnawed the inside of her cheek, trying to think. It was such a fantastic opportunity! She could barely contain her excitement, yet, at the same time, there was so much to consider.

"I don't think I could work here," she mused aloud.

He laughed. "I should say not! I wouldn't allow you to be ogled all day by that wild bunch out there! No way. I already have to face the fact that Cooper has the hots for you." He moved to face her, leaning against the desk and crossing his ankles stretched out in front of him. By his wide smile she knew he was only teasing her about Jim.

"What I had in mind," he continued, "was for you to work at home. I honestly feel that you should be at home with Allison during this critical time in her development. But I fully understand your need to work. You could set your own hours, work when you wanted to, but be there with her all day. How does that sound?"

"It would be wonderful, Jace. I worried about being away from her so much too, before . . . well, before we married."

"Great. Then it's all settled."

"Wait! Let me think a minute." In concentration she tapped her index finger against pursed lips. "Wouldn't I have to work closely with the production crews?"

"Very good question. A television station in Houston is supplying us with production facilities. They'll do all the dirty work after you turn over the scripts. If they should need you, they can always call. Or if necessary, you could take the company plane down there for a day or two."

"Oh, Jace, it sounds too good to be true."

"It's only a matter of your wanting to do it. I know you're qualified." He stroked her cheek gently and smiled at her confidently. "Shall I call Willoughby and tell him he's got a new employee?"

She hesitated only an instant then clapped her hands. "Yes, Yes!"

꧁ ꧂

Katherine and Jace agreed to stay and share lunch with the roughnecks. One of them had driven into town and bought hamburgers and french fries. After her noon bottle of milk, Allison seemed content to snooze in the crook of Billy's arm. He was impervious to the ribbing he received from his cohorts.

The drill bit rumbled as it ate its way through earth and rock, and the throbbing motor that propelled it deep into the ground kept up a cadence that Katherine was sure would drive her mad if she had to listen to it for hours on end. But the roughnecks were oblivious to the noise as they rapidly consumed a tremendous amount of food.

They sat on the ground or in pick-up truck beds, or stood in small groups. There was much jocularity among them. Sometimes their language became ribald, but Katherine felt that it had been cleaned up considerably on her behalf.

When everyone was finished eating, Jace shouted

above the noise, "What in the hell is going on here? Do you think because I've brought my wife to meet you that you can slough off the rest of the day? Everyone back to work. The picnic's over." His voice sounded stern, but he was smiling. There were grumbles and grimaces, but all of them ambled back to their jobs. Many of them saluted obsequiously or spoke shyly to Katherine as they passed her. Jim Cooper smiled broadly at her from under his hard hat, but hustled back to work when Jace glared at him through squinting eyes.

The Manning family left a short time later. When they were climbing the stairs to the front door of the apartment, Jace said, "You'll get a package from Willoughby in the next few days. He's going to send some material that you may find useful. It will include a lot of dry facts and figures, but some human interest stories too."

"I'm anxious to get started." She paused with her hand on the banister. "I almost forgot. I'll have to notify someone at the college that I'm not coming back, won't I?"

Jace stood aside and let her go in ahead of him after he opened the door. He was grinning mysteriously, and she detected a glint in his blue eyes. A moment later she knew why he was so pleased with himself.

Resting on a new desk parked in the middle of the living room was a new electric typewriter. Katherine squealed in delight and spun her head around to look at him in surprise. "For me?" she cried.

"No, for Allison," he said dryly.

She ignored his derision and hurried across the room to inspect the splendid piece of machinery. It had every conceivable gadget, an automatic correcting system, and features that would intimidate Katherine before she learned how to use them.

"Oh, Jace, it's wonderful. I . . . when?"

"I bought it two days ago and asked that it be delivered while we were gone. I wanted it to be a surprise. Do you like it?"

"Like it? It's a writer's dream. If you could see—" She broke off when a thought occurred to her. She looked at him through slitted green eyes. "You were pretty confident that I'd accept your job, weren't you?"

He laughed. "I hoped you would."

She tried to remain miffed, but couldn't, and broke into an exultant smile. "I should be mad at you for taking me for granted, but I can't be. Thank you, Jace, for everything. The job. The typewriter. Everything." She felt humbled and ashamed that she had ever doubted his motives.

"Come here and thank me properly. With a kiss." He was staring hard at her, his easy smile gone.

Suddenly unnerved by his tone of voice, Katherine forced her reluctant legs to walk toward him. He had taken Allison from her when she had rushed across the room to inspect her gift. The baby lay contentedly in his arms. Katherine stood on tiptoes and raised her lips to his cheek, kissing it lightly.

He frowned as she pulled back. "That's not a kiss. This is a kiss."

He leaned down and captured her mouth with his. Unable to hold her in his arms because of Allison, he used other means. The force of his kiss was far stronger and more compelling than any physical hold could have been.

His firm lips moved over hers with tantalizing non-commitment. He nibbled at her lower lip until Katherine opened it to permit him entry. Still he refrained, exploring her lips with a lazy tongue.

She moaned and moved closer, clasping him around the neck with both hands and forcing his head lower. Only then did he satisfy her longing. His mouth took hers with a sweet violence. His kiss made her body sing with sensations that touched her soul.

With a detached part of her brain, Katherine asked herself how he was able to so effortlessly render her completely helpless. *How does he command my senses so totally? I mustn't surrender to what I'm feeling. But I want to. I want him.*

These thoughts raced through her mind even as she drank the nectar of his mouth. Then Jace moved his head and discovered a new region of her mouth to explore, and all other thoughts were banished.

Katherine felt the pummeling fists on her chest and only then did she realize that Allison was crushed between them. She dropped her arms from Jace's neck and slowly backed away.

They looked down at the offended baby lying between them. The infant face crumpled in indignation, and Allison began to squall loudly.

"Now look what we've done," Jace said. Placatingly, he raised Allison to his shoulder and patted her back. "Come on, princess, I'll make it all up to you." As he went into the kitchen, he said over his shoulder, "I'll feed her. You play with your new toy."

Katherine didn't argue. She sat at the new desk and picked up the instruction booklet.

"This manual looks like an encyclopedia," she called into the kitchen. "I'm going to have to study for hours before I'll feel adequate to even turn the typewriter on."

"You can handle it," Jace called back.

Almost an hour had passed before Katherine was roused from her absorption in the instruction manual. Jace was carrying Allison through the living room on the way to her bedroom. "She's fed. I even managed to get most of that disgusting-looking stuff in her mouth. She kept me company while I made a batch of my famous spaghetti sauce. Is that okay with you?"

"Sounds delicious."

"It needs to simmer for a while. You stay where you are and I'll put Allison to bed."

By the time he finished the sentence, Katherine was again bent over the typewriter, lost in its many intricacies.

A startled cry of pain jolted her out of her diligent study. She dropped the heavy book and ran toward the bedroom.

Chapter Nine

꙰ ꙰

Katherine swung open the door and flew into the room. It was empty. She stared at the vacant crib stupidly until she heard another sharp gasp and a vicious "Ouch!" before realizing that Jace's cries were coming from the bathroom.

Katherine hurried to the doorway. She halted abruptly, frozen in astonishment.

Jace and Allison were in the bathtub. The contrast of Allison's smooth, white bottom against Jace's dark, hair-matted chest was startling. Even more startling to Katherine was the sight of Jace's naked body submerged in the warm water as he reclined in the bathtub. Even his knees, raised to accommodate his long body in the short tub, didn't screen his masculinity from her amazed and involuntarily curious eyes.

"Oh, Katherine, thank God. Help me." Jace winced in pain, and, for the first time, she noted the source of his distress.

Allison was lying on her stomach along his chest. Each of her tiny, plump fists was clamped around a handful of the hair on Jace's chest. In her excitement over finding this rare new toy, Allison's fists were clenching tighter each second. Her small legs were kicking against his flat stomach in delight.

Katherine swallowed the large lump that was blocking her breathing passages and murmured, "I'll just get her off . . ." She leaned down and grasped the wet, wriggling body around her chubby waist.

"No!" Jace exclaimed in panic. "If you do that, I'll be depilated, and that tends to smart."

Katherine looked at the tiny fingers which seemed helplessly enmeshed in the dark hair and saw that he was right.

"What—?" she started to ask.

"See if you can unwind the hair from around her fingers. I'm afraid to let go of her. She's as slippery as an eel."

Katherine closed her eyes for a moment and drew a deep, restorative breath. Then she knelt down beside the bathtub. She worked the small fingers of Allison's hand until they relaxed and released their grip on the crisp, wet curls. When the first fist was free, Jace reached up and grasped it, holding it away from him.

Katherine worked with the other fist, leaning over his body in order to see what she was doing. She refused to feel the breath that stirred her hair as her head was bent close to his chin.

Finally, Jace was free from Allison's painful grip, but instead of handing her over to an anxious Katherine, he quickly stood up with the baby still in his arms.

"I ought to spank you for that, young lady," Jace chided Allison. "From now on when we take a bath together, I'll wear a T-shirt."

Immodestly, he walked naked into the bedroom, still carrying Allison and drying her with a soft towel. He ignored Katherine after saying "Thanks, honey" over his retreating shoulder.

Katherine skirted by him as she went through the bedroom. He was dressing Allison in her pajamas as he leaned over the crib. His taut hips were only one shade lighter than his broad, smooth back. They tapered from his narrow waist into long, muscled thighs. Katherine hurried through the door into the living room.

She fumbled with the manual which a few moments ago had so engrossed her and her trembling hand had dropped it on the floor before Katherine placed it beside the typewriter. She couldn't resume studying. Of that she was certain. Her eyes weren't able to focus properly. She kept seeing the image of Jace as he lay back in the bathtub.

She went into the kitchen. Something in there would distract her, calm her down, she hoped, so that she could start acting like a rational person again and not a quivering blob of jelly.

She raised the lid on the pan of simmering spaghetti sauce and sniffed the delicious aroma. She was replacing the lid when she heard soft footfalls and knew that Jace was standing behind her. She dropped the aluminum lid, and it clattered onto the range.

Before she could retrieve it, one of Jace's arms came from under her arm, picked up the lid, and replaced it securely on the pan. She felt his chest pressed against her back.

His other arm came from behind her to join the first. He slipped both under her blouse, and, with one swift motion, unclasped the front fastener of her bra. Pushing aside the wisp of lace and nylon, he cupped her breasts in his hands.

"It got you all hot and bothered, didn't it?" He was nuzzling the back of her neck under her hair. The tip of his tongue explored the velvet smooth skin behind her ear.

"What?" she croaked. His hands were kneading her gently, then flattening her with pressing palms.

"The sight of my nakedness. It's been known to cause quite a disturbance. Why, when I was in Africa, the sight of me walking down the street was enough to make the parents of nubile daughters tremble in fear." His voice was barely above a whisper, entrancing. He moved closer, and his thighs rubbed against the backs of her legs and hips.

It was hard to articulate anything, but Katherine kept up the inane conversation. "Y-you walked naked down the street?"

His hands pushed her breasts together, forming a deep cleavage, and he raked his thumbs over the aroused nipples.

"Of course. In some African cultures that's a matter of form. No pun intended." He caught her earlobe between his teeth.

"Well, this isn't Africa." She sighed as his hands moved over the flat planes of her stomach. "And I'll thank you not to . . . oh, Jace."

He turned her to face him. The cerulean eyes were full of resolve as he lifted her and carried her through the living room to the bedroom which, until now, had been used exclusively by him.

Gently and carefully he lowered her onto the king-size bed. He stood up and whipped the towel from around his waist, dropping it to the floor as he lay down beside Katherine.

He smoothed back the hair from her flushed cheeks and brushed light kisses on her temple. "Katherine, I'm going to make love to you." He wasn't asking permission. It was a statement of intention. He kissed her tenderly, drawing on her tongue with persuasive insistence.

He gloried in each part of her body as it was revealed

to him. He removed her clothing with practiced skill and maddening leisure, frequently stopping to nibble and caress.

When he eased the bikini panties down her long slender legs, he whispered endearments in praise of her body that Katherine could never have imagined coming from anyone's lips.

He stretched out beside her and held her tightly against him. Slowly the tension in her body ebbed under the soothing strokes of his fingers. Their arousing exploration coaxed her to participate. Her head was thrown back against the pillow, her chin raised, allowing his seeking mouth access to her throat.

His lips settled on her mouth, kissing it with infinite passion and tenderness. His tongue searched its sweetness even as his hands traversed her body. His lips were still resting on hers as he whispered, ''I don't know what you like. Tell me if—'' She sealed his words inside by capturing his lips with her own. If this were an example of things to come, there was nothing she wouldn't like.

His mouth trailed across her cheek to her ear and teased it with soft, warm breath and a darting tongue.

His hand caressed her from her shoulders, across her breasts, and around her waist. His fingers stroked the silkiness of her inner thighs, and a liquid fire ran through her from his fingertips to the very center of her being.

''Your skin is like velvet,'' he murmured. He eased

his hand back and forth across her feminine cradle. "Remember the night I put you to bed?"

"Yes, Jace," she breathed. His hands were a vivid reminder.

"I wanted to touch you like this then." He rested his hand on the soft tuft at the top of her legs. "I'm glad there's nothing between us now."

Her ragged breath was trapped inside her mouth by his plundering kiss. She clasped his head on either side of his jaw just under his ears and moved his head downward.

"Jace," she pleaded, "kiss me here." She placed his head against her breasts.

He kissed the soft curves. His tongue outlined their undersides until she was writhing with longing. When she felt his mouth close around her nipple, she heard herself moan in ecstasy. He pulled on her gently, then raised his head slightly and used only his tongue to assuage the aching bud.

She clasped his shoulders and explored the hard muscles under her fingers. She became braver and slid her hands between their bodies, combing her fingertips through the hair on his chest and curiously examining the small brown nipples nestled in it. It delighted her to hear his quickening breath.

"Ah, Katherine, you're so sweet," he said as his fingers discovered the moist warmth between her thighs. Her sighs echoed his.

"Now?" he asked with lips that nibbled hers. "Now?"

She nodded and his plunging kiss was symbolic.

He raised himself above her and found the treasure he sought. He fit his strength into her softness and applied a gentle pressure. When he met the unexpected veil of resistance, he paused and looked down at her with a bewildered expression. The urgent hands on the back of his thighs and her arching hips entreated him not to linger in his purpose.

The initial pain vanished, and Katherine submitted to the thrill of the experience. She blocked out every conscious thought, anything that would dim the lightning fury of the sensations washing over her. It no longer mattered what his name was, or who he was related to, or that they came from different worlds. All that had import was that her body was one with his. It was not only a physical fusion, but one of the spirit as well. She belonged; it was right.

Even though he was the first, Katherine knew him to be expert. He encouraged her, praised her, adored her, made love to her with words as well as his body. He kissed, nibbled, licked, caressed, stroked, breathed her. It went beyond mere consummation.

When she felt herself slipping into some uncharted but seductive oblivion, she cried, "Jace! Jace!"

"Yes, darling, yes," he whispered in her ear. "Katherine, sweet Katherine, give in to it."

And she did.

"A virgin?" Jace asked in awe as they lay side by side, holding each other close. "I'm married to a twenty-seven-year-old virgin." He shook his head at the wonder of it all.

"Not anymore," sang Katherine as she snuggled closer to him, if that were possible.

"Hussy!" He slapped her naked bottom playfully. "Now I suppose you'll be wanting to do this all the time," he sighed in feigned resignation.

She giggled and supported herself on her elbows while covering his face with wet, smacking kisses. He began tickling her ribs until she fell backward, and moments later she collapsed helplessly under his weight. He looked down into her face and laughed softly before taking her mouth with his.

Locking her hands behind his neck, Katherine drew him closer to her, welcoming their return to passion. He stroked her neck and moved his questing fingers to her chest before settling them possessively on her breasts.

He drew back from his ardent kiss and gazed at her breasts even as his fingers traced a path of arousal. He watched as the nipples tautened under his manipulation. "Fascinating," he declared as he leaned down and kissed them gently.

His hand moved lower onto her flattened abdomen. Just then Katherine's stomach growled ominously. Jace chuckled, "Are you hungry?" He pulled away from her.

"Yes," Katherine groaned, straining toward him. The inches between them seemed to stretch into a gulf. "But not for food."

"Come on," he said getting up from the bed. "Let's eat." He pulled on a pair of gym shorts and a T-shirt that covered only his shoulders and the top half of his chest, leaving his midriff bare. "I'll be offended if you don't do justice to my highly acclaimed spaghetti sauce."

"I'd rather stay in bed," whined Katherine.

"So would I, but from now on, Mrs. Manning, I'm going to make sure that you retain a high energy level. You expend it in such a marvelous way." He grabbed her arm and dragged her up to her knees on the side of the bed. He buried his face in her neck as he held her close, moving his hands up and down her back.

"Katherine?"

"Hmm?"

"Do me a favor?"

"Uh-huh."

"Wear that shirt you had on the first day I came here. Your painting shirt. Tie it up the way you had it then. Okay?"

She pulled away from him and looked into the glinting blue eyes. "That's the favor?" she asked.

"Not all of it," he admitted mischievously. "Don't wear anything else except bikini panties."

"Jace!" she huffed. "That's indecent."

"So? I'm not going to tell anybody. Are you?"

"You're incorrigible," she whispered, planting a kiss in one of the dimples beside his mouth.

"And you love it," he answered huskily. Then he pushed her unceremoniously backward on the bed and said, "Hurry up. I'm hungry too."

When Katherine joined him in the kitchen wearing the prescribed outfit, he turned to face her and appraised her lecherously. He came to her, folded her in an encompassing embrace, and kissed her thoroughly.

"That's what I wanted to do that first day," he said.

"That's what you *did* that first day," she reminded him dryly.

"Oh, yeah. I did, didn't I? Well, good for me." He grinned.

While the spaghetti was boiling, Katherine tossed together a salad, and Jace spread thick slices of French bread with garlic butter and popped them into the oven.

With an alacrity born of practice, he opened a bottle of red wine that he had put in the refrigerator earlier to chill. Miraculously, everything was ready at the same time and they sat down to eat their late dinner.

Was the meal especially delicious, or was it Katherine's happiness that made it seem to be? They chatted continually. The meal stretched over two hours.

She learned that Jace would be thirty-three on his next birthday and what that date was. His middle name was Lawrence. They shared stories of their youth. Each learned the other's likes and dislikes, prejudices, political inclinations, and personal philosophies.

When they were replete with spaghetti, salad, bread, and wine, Jace insisted that they each have a bowl of chocolate ice cream. As they companionably shared the chore of cleaning up, Katherine marveled again that he was able to eat so much and still retain a physique that sported not one ounce of fat.

They stood side by side at Allison's crib, arms around each other's waists, and felt drawn even closer by the commitment they shared to rear the child to be a responsible, compassionate human being. Katherine changed Allison's diaper, but the baby didn't awaken.

There was no question as to where Katherine was sleeping that night. She went with Jace into the other bedroom naturally and uninhibitedly. Before she had time to straighten the linens on the bed, he had stripped out of his clothes and reached for her. With meticulous care he untied the knot under her bosom and pulled the shirt from her shoulders. She stepped out of her panties as they lay down together on the wide bed.

"I'm insanely jealous," Jace said as he stroked her shoulder.

"Why?" she asked in a voice that sounded more like a contented purr.

"Because the first time you were on this bed, you were with Cooper."

"Yes," she sighed with pretended despair, "I suppose I'll have to give Jim up."

They laughed, then were quiet for a long moment, enraptured with holding each other.

"How do you feel?" Jace whispered into the darkness.

"Like this," Katherine returned impishly. Shyly, she lowered her hand under the covers. He inhaled sharply with a soft hiss when she found her target. She smiled in satisfaction at his instantaneous stirring under her fingertips.

"Oh, God," he moaned. "That wasn't exactly what I meant, but your answer will suffice." With an effort he tried to control his rapid breathing. "Actually, I wondered if I had hurt you. I wasn't very gentle." He groaned when she became more confident. "Katherine . . ." he rasped. Then more levelly, "It never occurred to me that you might be a virgin."

"Did you think I was a liberated, promiscuous swinger trailing a string of forsaken lovers behind me?" She nibbled at the base of his throat.

"No, of course not," he ground out between clenched teeth. Speech was becoming more difficult with each passing second. "I just thought that surely someone as beautiful as you would have been . . . involved . . . before now. I'm delighted to learn you weren't."

"Oh, Jace," she murmured as she buried her face in

the hair on his chest and brushed it with butterfly kisses. Lightly, she flicked her tongue over his nipples.

"Katherine—" he cried softly. "You . . . you take me to heaven." He reached under the sheet and lifted her hand away from him, bringing it to his lips. He pressed a passionate kiss into her palm even as he rolled her gently onto her back.

Masterfully controlling the urgency she had induced, it was with utmost gentleness that he took her once again to blissful completion.

The following weeks were idyllic. Katherine and Jace were totally engrossed in each other. They shared those looks and touches that, to lovers, are secret, and yet broadcast their affection to anyone who chanced to intercept these transmissions.

They laughed, talked, and made love with a joy that belied the strained circumstances of their marriage. Katherine tinkered with and experimented on her new typewriter, and, by the end of the first week, was composing rough drafts for her first series of commercials.

During the day while Jace was at the drilling site, she spent long hours jotting down ideas and doing research. She read her drafts aloud to Allison, who was a captive audience. The baby was relegated to a pallet on the living room floor until one evening when Jace brought in an indoor swing. As he wound up the A-shaped contraption and placed Allison in the comfortable cloth seat, he remarked, "This apartment is shrinking more each day."

For one who had always cooked out of necessity, Katherine discovered an uncharacteristic joy in cooking for Jace. One night she surprised him with a chocolate pie, which he had emphatically insisted was his favorite food.

She knew him to have a vicious temper. Hadn't she witnessed it the night Ronald Welsh attacked her? It had surfaced briefly in some of the arguments before their marriage. On the day they went to the lake and she inadvertently compared him to Peter she realized just how explosive his temper could be.

But there was no evidence of it now. He was easy to live with, neat to a fault, and generous. Allison enjoyed an abundance of affection from him. Every day he came in from work, showered and changed, and then spent time talking to and playing with her. Sometimes, if she were fussy, he would just rock her. His attention always seemed to pacify her.

Katherine overheard him cooing to her as he rocked her in the wicker chair one evening. "Allison, sweet baby girl, Daddy loves you. I love you, Allison."

The words pierced Katherine's heart. For even in their highest moments of passion, Jace had never hinted that he loved her. He showered her with love words, and his lovemaking was definitely a sharing experience. Never did he appease his desire without patiently and tenderly bringing her with him to perfect satisfaction.

She suddenly longed to hear those three words spoken to her with the same open sincerity that he was speaking them to Allison. And then she knew.

She loved Jason Manning.

When had it happened? At what point had she thrown off the cloak of suspicion and accepted him as the forthright person he seemed to be? When had she stopped searching the depths of his eyes for hidden motives? She didn't know. All she knew was that she loved him and that should he not remain a part of her life, it would become a vacuum, a dark void.

Never had she allowed herself such vulnerability to another human being. It was a frightening submission. He had first gained control of her life. Now he had control of her heart and emotions as well. What would she do if he betrayed that trust? How could she ever cope with duplicity from him now?

She pushed the terrifying thought from her mind as she listened to him softly singing to Allison. He wouldn't betray her. He couldn't! Not after they had experienced such an all-consuming sexual union. Their appetites for each other had been insatiable and they had not been left unassuaged.

Another nasty thought invaded her mind. Lust. Men could enjoy sex while keeping their hearts and minds detached. Is that all their glorious lovemaking meant to Jace? Was he so adept at sex that he could make her believe it meant as much to him as it did to her? Were the words he passionately whispered in her ear only rehearsed recitations?

"Hey, what imaginative culinary delight have you concocted for our dinner tonight?"

Jace brought her out of her disturbing reverie as he came up behind her at the kitchen stove and placed his hands on her shoulders.

"Lizard eyes," she said, laughing, and unconsciously settling her bottom against the fly of his jeans.

"With cheese sauce? Great! One of my favorites." He nuzzled her neck and thrust his hips against hers suggestively. "What's for dessert?"

Take one day at a time, Katherine, she told herself. *He couldn't kiss you like this if he didn't feel some measure of affection for you.*

As the kiss deepened, all other thoughts were dispelled.

Katherine cursed the potholes that jarred her new car and made it rattle as she negotiated the road that led out to the dri!'¬g site. She was surprising Jace with a special lunch. Happy had been all too agreeable to watch Allison when Katherine told her of her plans.

Happy Cooper was sensitive to the change in the relationship between Jace and Katherine. She had suspected since his first appearance that he was Katherine's husband. She guessed he had come after Katherine when she left over some lover's quarrel.

Anyone could see that they were crazy about each other. And, surely, Jace was Allison's father. He couldn't be any more enamored with that baby. She was exultant that these two young people had patched up whatever differences had driven them apart in the first place. Maybe they had not had enough time alone together. She made it her personal duty to see that that didn't happen again by volunteering to baby-sit with Allison at every opportunity. Besides, now that Katherine was working at home, she missed having Allison at her house each day.

Katherine could hear the cacophony surrounding the drilling rig before she reached it. Relieved that her jostling journey was over, she parked her car a short distance from the site and walked the rest of the way.

A bottle of wine, chicken salad, and fruit were in the basket under her arm. Her breasts, unrestrained by a bra, swayed under her silk blouse as she walked over the rough ground. She giggled in anticipation. Yes, Jace would enjoy this lunch break. But they must have privacy. She mulled over several devices to get Billy out of the trailer while she and Jace enjoyed an intimate lunch.

To her surprise she saw that it wouldn't be necessary for them to get rid of Billy. He wasn't in the trailer, but tinkering with one of the battered pick-up trucks. By the look of all the parts lying on the ground around him, he would be busy for quite some time.

"Hello, Billy," she called over the noise.

When he looked up and saw her, he glanced nervously over his shoulder toward the trailer and then shuffled toward her on his bowed legs, wiping his hands on an oil-soaked rag.

"Hello, Katherine."

"Why aren't you working in the trailer? Did Jace put you onto another project?" She laughed, indicating the disemboweled pick-up.

"No, I left the trailer on my own accord. I didn't want to be under the same roof with *her*." He nodded toward a shiny, long Winnebago that Katherine hadn't noticed before.

"Her?" she asked curiously.

"Yeah," was Billy's only comment before he turned his head and disdainfully spat a stream of tobacco juice into the dirt.

He ambled back to the truck and Katherine looked in bemusement at the motor home and then to the trailer.

"Oh, well," she sighed. "So much for surprise lunches."

She went to the trailer, opened the door, and stepped

into :' : dim interior. After allowing her eyes to adjust from the bright sunlight outside, she looked toward Jace's desk.

Her heart plummeted to the floor. She stood speechless, stunned, and heartbroken. Then hot, angry jealousy suffused her whole body.

Jace was leaning against his desk. His long legs were spread wide and stretched out in front of him. Between them, standing with her middle pressed intimately against him, was a dark-haired woman. Jace's hands were locked behind her back. Her red laquered fingertips were ruffling through his thick, black hair.

At Jace's startled reaction to Katherine's entrance, the woman turned toward her and stared haughtily with dark, liquid eyes. She didn't release her hold on Jace. Instead, with silky, gushing tones she said, "This must be Katherine. What a pleasure to meet you." Sensuously she moved closer to Jace and said with feigned embarrassment, "Oh, forgive me. I didn't introduce myself. I'm Lacey Newton Manning. Jace's wife."

Chapter Ten

Katherine must have drawn on some surplus
of discipline and self-control to keep herself
from either fainting or fleeing. Instead her
hands clenched into painful fists at her sides,
her nails digging into her palms. Her lungs constricted.
The breath seemed to leave her body by slow degrees
until she gasped in an effort to sustain herself.

She tore her eyes from Lacey's triumphant mocking
face to Jace's. His frustration was manifested in the
slight twitch in his rigid jaw and the hard, implacable
eyes. Slowly, he extricated himself from Lacey's embrace and stood up, pushing her away from him.

"That's not exactly accurate, Lacey. You are my *ex*-wife. A pertinent distinction, I think," he corrected.

So, he really had been married to this woman, Katherine thought. She had been clinging to a tenuous thread of hope that perhaps this Lacey was playing a practical joke on an old friend. But the pouting, seductive expression the brunette bestowed on Jace denoted that their relationship went far beyond friendship. Even a fool could see that.

"Oh, Jace," Lacey chided petulantly, "you always were annoyingly precise. I still *feel* married to you. I'll always consider you to be my husband. In the eyes of God, we're married."

"Oh?" Jace cocked a skeptical eyebrow. "Lacey, if God looks upon everyone who has carnal knowledge of another to be married, the world is overpopulated with bigamists." Katherine never recalled Jace sounding so bitter. Was he referring to their marriage? The pain in her heart was unbearable.

He continued to stare at Lacey closely, while she returned his look with an open invitation on her provocative lips.

Katherine felt alien and useless. She had to get out. Their intimate looks sickened her. She had interrupted a private interlude which they seemed eager to resume.

The picnic basket fell noisily to the floor. Spitefully, Katherine hoped everything would spill out and make a big mess. Maybe the wine bottle would break. As her hand touched the doorknob, Jace barked, "Katherine, where are you going?"

She looked at him with angry incredulity. Had he gone mad? Did he think she was going to stand here and witness his lust for—or love for—his former wife?

"I'm going home," she stated coldly. "I only came out to bring you some lunch."

"Now isn't that—" Lacey started, but Jace cut her off.

"Thank you," he said. His face hadn't lost that harried look, but his perception never failed. He raked her body quickly with intuitive eyes. He knew her purpose for surprising him, and she flushed hotly. Her plans for an affectionate playtime between a husband and wife now seemed obscene.

"Maybe we can share it later," he suggested.

"I don't think so," Katherine returned sharply.

Jace muttered an expletive under his breath. Every line and angle of his body radiated his agitation. "Well, don't leave yet. I want to talk to you."

Lacey hopped up onto the desk and crossed her legs. Her blue silk slacks tightly contoured her hips and legs. Through her beige crocheted top, Katherine could plainly see her lush, coral-tipped breasts. Jace, she thought miserably, could see them too.

"Isn't Jace a dear husband, Katherine?" she purred. "When we were married, he barely left me alone for an hour at a time."

"Lacey," Jace grated.

"I still remember each time we made love, which was often," she laughed. "He makes sex an event, doesn't he?"

Katherine felt the bile rising at the back of her throat and longed to rush for the door and put as much distance as possible between her and those mocking brown eyes and sensuous mouth.

"Of course, ours was a love match and yours . . ." her cooing voice trailed off meaningfully. Katherine's mind caustically completed the sentence. Had Jace found it necessary to explain the circumstances surrounding his hasty marriage to Lacey?

"Lacey, you're dwelling on the past and that doesn't concern Katherine in the least." Was there a trace of warning in Jace's tone?

"Oh, on the contrary, darling." Lacey placed her hands on either side of her on the desk and leaned forward. Her heavy breasts dangled in front of her like luscious ripe melons. "I think Katherine would find it extremely interesting to learn that we divorced over the topic of children."

She took her eyes off of Jace and settled them on Katherine condescendingly. "You see, Jace has this big hang-up about families. As soon as we married, he started in on me to have babies." She pouted. "I wanted him all to myself for a while."

"Lacey, I'm—"

She leaned back negligently and swung her legs back

and forth in front of the desk like a pendulum. She ignored Jace's threatening interruption and continued, unaffected by his growing anger.

"Isn't it lucky that he acquired a ready-made family by marrying you?" Her smile was brilliant, revealing sharp white teeth.

Katherine gnawed her lower lip. She refused to allow herself to break down in front of Lacey or Jace. When he made a move toward her, she jerked away from him. Everything Lacey was saying was the truth, but somehow hearing it verbalized by this gorgeous woman who had been married to Jace, lived with him, slept—

Katherine shuddered. That he must have told Lacey about their personal life was an unforgivable insult. Maybe she was standing here listening to Lacey because she subconsciously sought punishment. She had been foolish to get into this marriage in the first place. Then she had gone one step further and fallen in love with Jace when she knew it was hopeless. She had come to trust him. That was her most ruinous mistake. She should have known better. Hadn't Mary loved and trusted Peter too?

"Knowing how Jace loves the family image and all, how could he not volunteer to rear poor, dear Peter's little baby girl? However, it's just like Jace to sacrifice everything for a noble cause."

"Shut up, Lacey." Jace turned toward the woman and impaled her with blue eyes that were sparking with anger. Naturally he was angry. Lacey was pointing out the unfortunate details of his marriage, and they rankled him, especially since he was obviously still in love with his ex-wife.

"Well, leave it to you, darling, to make the best of a bad situation." Lacey studied her manicured fingertips with absorbing concentration. "I mean getting Katherine that little job of hers was so generous of you. Of course, the busier you keep her, the less time you'll have to spend with her."

Lacey's last words pierced Katherine like a spear. Involuntarily her muscles twitched, and she turned to Jace in fury. "You!" she cried. "What did you do to get me my job?"

"Oh, my dear, if only you could have heard him selling Daddy on the idea," Lacey drawled. "I listened on the other phone. Why Jace was practically begging Daddy to go along with the idea of these silly commercials."

Katherine listened to every word, aghast at their implication. She searched Jace's face for some sign of denial, but his only reaction was a clenching jaw and hardening blue diamond eyes.

"Is that true, Jace?" She strangled on her words. "Is it true that you contrived an unnecessary job for me?"

"Katherine, please listen—" he took a step toward her.

"Answer me, damn you," she fairly screamed. "Did Mr. Newton come up with the idea or did you?"

"You don't understand—"

"Tell me. Now!"

"Godammit!" he exploded. "I would explain if you'd let me finish a sentence."

"I don't want any of your glib explanations," she said succinctly. "Whose idea were the commercials?" When he still didn't reply, she shouted, "Whose?"

"Mine!" he roared.

His volume matched hers and the word ricocheted off the walls of the trailer, echoing in the small confines of the interior.

Katherine and Jace faced each other like wild, raging bulls. Their chests heaved, their nostrils flared, their anger consumed them.

Finally Katherine forced the pent-up tension out of her body. She straightened her shoulders and turned to leave the trailer. She swung open the door and stepped out onto the low step.

It surprised her when Jace followed close on her heels. He grabbed her upper arm in a viselike grip.

"Let go of me," she snarled, trying to pull her arm free.

"Not a chance. You aren't about to go running out of here like a she-devil out for revenge. That would start tongues wagging for sure."

He walked close to her. She stumbled to keep pace with his long, angry strides. "Well, we sure wouldn't want any adverse gossip about the boss's love life,

185

would we?'' she asked sweetly. "I think your caution is a trifle ludicrous when your ex-wife has already arrived in a mobile bedroom.''

His grip on her arm was painful, but he tightened it even more. He ignored her sarcasm and asked, "Where in the hell is your car?''

"Over there,'' she indicated the station wagon parked under an oak tree at the edge of the woods.

He practically dragged her the rest of the way over the stony ground. Did he think he was fooling his men with this display of husbandly chivalry? Couldn't they tell by his rigid face and ramrod straight back that he was furious?

When he reached the car and was out of earshot from anyone who might be able to hear over the noisy equipment, he leaned down and said, "Nothing that was said or done back there has any relevance to us. Do you hear me, Katherine?'' He shook her slightly.

"You're hurting my arm. Will you please let go?'' She looked at him levelly, revealing none of the torment she was feeling inside.

He released her immediately, and she rubbed her arm, trying to restore circulation. "Should I expect rougher treatment when you get home? Or *are* you coming home?''

"Katherine,'' he ground out in exasperation. He looked away from her, out across the landscape that was incongruously peaceful. He sighed deeply and returned his gaze to her. "When I got you the job—''

"Thanks for nothing," she said bitterly.

"I was doing it for you!" he flared.

She laughed harshly. "Oh, sure you were." Her green eyes hardened as she said, "That was the only area of my life where you weren't in control. My career. You took over my life, my house, my . . ." She broke off before she made an admission that would confirm her absolute humiliation. "You had to have it all, didn't you? You wouldn't let me retain even a fragment of my pride or self-respect. God! You Mannings are greedy. Now I'm in your debt and under your supervision completely, aren't I?"

She recognized the symptoms. His temper was rising to the surface. Her words penetrated the armor. *So*, Katherine thought as she watched the lines around his mouth become more deeply etched, *I was right. The truth always hurts, and he can't take it*.

"Okay," he said menacingly. "Believe what you will, Katherine." He took one step closer to her. "But there's one other thing I control that you failed to mention."

"W-what?" she asked tremulously, instinctively afraid of the predatory gleam in his azure eyes.

"This," he said, reaching for her and drawing her to him.

"No—" she protested before he covered her mouth with his.

After a punishing kiss, he lifted his head for a moment. "You can start paying back all those debts you owe me,'' he taunted. His arms held her immobile against his hard, unyielding body. He pressed his lips against her closed mouth and wouldn't give up the bruising pressure until she had opened it to him.

His tongue forced its way in, plundering her mouth. His hips thrust against hers, pushing her into the side of the car. His hands were everywhere, insulting and abusive. Thankfully, his back was to the drilling site and no one could witness her debasement.

He left her mouth and buried his lips in her neck. ''You came out here for an intimate lunch together, didn't you?'' he asked in a gruff voice.

She whimpered, tears on the brink of her lids, as he reminded her of her original plans. So much had happened since then. How shattered were her dreams in the space of an hour!

''I would have liked that, Katherine.'' He settled one long, brown hand on her breast. ''I know you have nothing on under this blouse. In my mind, I can see your breasts, feel them, taste them.''

He found her mouth again, and this time there was no violence in his kiss. It was devastatingly tender. His mouth sensuously sipped at her lips, her tongue, until she relaxed the steely tautness of her body.

His thumbs brushed across her nipples through the fabric of her shirt until he felt them respond. They were like hard, smooth buttons under his touch.

Katherine felt herself slipping into submission. Her resolve melted under his caresses. Her body betrayed her by responding to him. No. She mustn't. From the first she had been drawn to him by his persuasive sexuality and flagrant virility. Now she was suffering for her weakness. This meant nothing to him. He only used these embraces as a means of decreasing her will, eliminating her self-control, getting his way.

Gleaning every ounce of depleting strength, she pushed him away from her. His eyes, glazed with passion, blinked rapidly, trying to focus. When he looked down into her angry, closed face, he dropped his arms to his sides.

"You're wrong, Jace. I'm no longer susceptible. You don't influence any part of my life. I'm leaving now. By the looks of things, Lacey intends to stay a while. I'm sure she's more than willing to satisfy your baser instincts."

She got in the car and slammed the door. After she turned on the motor and engaged the gears, Jace put a restraining hand on the door handle.

"It's a pretty speech and a good act, Katherine, but it won't wash." His anger was gone. His voice was level, convincing, and deadly accurate. "You still want me as much as I want you. I'll be home at the normal time."

❦ ❦

Katherine cursed Jace, her own vulnerability, and the top stair she bumped her toe on as she went into the

189

apartment. Thankfully, Happy's car hadn't been in the driveway. She must have taken Allison with her on some errand. That permitted Katherine a brief respite during which she could contemplate her problem and bandage her wounds.

It was out of character for her to throw herself across the king-size bed and give in to a torrent of tears. The cool, collected, and stable Katherine Adams rarely allowed her emotions to erupt so vehemently. But never had she felt so betrayed.

She hadn't even known about Jace's former marriage. For how long were he and Lacey married? When? Why did they divorce? Lacey said one reason was his desire for children before she was ready to make such a commitment. Was Jace's mind so twisted that he would marry Katherine and take care of Allison in order to punish Lacey for her refusal to bear his children when he had wanted them? Had that been his motivation in maneuvering this charade?

Clutching the pillow that smelled of him, she buried her face in its softness and sobbed his name. *Why did I fall in love with him?* she berated herself. She should have known better. Love like this didn't exist except in the minds of poets and dreamers. It couldn't survive in the actual world.

She couldn't remember her father's love, though she was sure he had been affectionately fond of her. Grace Adams, with the death of her husband, had suddenly inherited the responsibility of providing for her children and herself at a time before women could expect equal opportunities on the job market. Her love had been in the form of personal sacrifices in order that Katherine and Mary might have more. Only rarely had she found time or energy after a long day at the post office to fondle and pet and express her love to her little girls. If a time for loving was made available, Mary was usually the recipient of it, for she was the baby.

Katherine didn't blame her father for dying. Nor could she find fault with her mother. But she longed to be loved. Defensively, she had protected herself from entanglements that would provide only temporary loving care. From somewhere deep inside her, she knew she couldn't tolerate the pain of parting, of losing again someone she loved. Not until she met Jace Manning had she opened her heart so wide, had she let down her defenses long enough for someone to show her deep affection.

She and Mary had been companionable, and, if anyone had asked her, she would have declared that she loved her sister. It would be the truth. But it wasn't the same. She and Mary had never shared the intellectual exchanges that she and Jace had. His quick wit and keen sense of humor couldn't compare to Mary's appealing naivete. Jace had received her first real love, and now he had spurned it.

When the flow of tears was finally exhausted, Katherine straightened the bed and restored her face. Happy noticed that Katherine was unusually quiet when she returned Allison, but Katherine gave away none of her abysmal misery. A stoic, indifferent countenance would be her shield.

She prepared dinner, talking to herself as she did so. She argued her case, rehearsed each word. If—and that was a big if—Jace came home as he said he would, she would be ready to meet his fluid logic, which she knew to be more lethal than a sword.

Deliberately, she bathed and dressed with care. He wasn't going to find her disheveled and distressed. There would be no humble groveling. She would defeat him with her aplomb.

Despite all the arguments that she didn't care if he came back or not, her heart lurched when she heard the distinctive clatter of the jeep's motor followed by his booted footsteps on the stairs.

She was winding up Allison's swing when he walked through the door. She gave him a cursory glance and then returned her attention to settling Allison comfortably in the canvas seat. Allison spotted Jace and started kicking her chubby legs and squealing delightedly. Katherine gave them her back and marched resentfully into the kitchen.

Jace behaved with aggravating normalcy. He cleaned up and played with Allison before dinner just as he always did. The longer she worked in the kitchen, the louder Katherine clanged the pots and pans together. When she burned her hand while impatiently extracting a sheet of rolls out of the oven without the protection of a potholder, she cursed loudly and crudely. *Damn him!* she thought. *He's reduced me to this!*

Jace strolled into the kitchen and asked politely, "Anything I can do?"

"No," she replied shortly. "I can do everything by myself," she said significantly.

"Okay," he said cheerfully and sat down at the table.

He was the picture of composedness as he sat at the table with his long legs stretched out in front of him, his ankles crossed, his arms folded across his chest. She had an overpowering impulse to dump a bowl of hot potatoes on top of his head just to see his insouciance destroyed.

He had put Allison down for the night, and they ate in silence—Jace with relish and appreciation, Katherine with a choking determination.

As usual, Jace helped her with the dishes. She avoided any contact with him. Once he put his hand into the warm soapy water and captured her hand. He stroked her palm with his thumb as he analyzed the storm in her green eyes. She angrily jerked her hand back to show him her aversion, but only succeeded in splashing sudsy water in her own face.

"I want to talk to you," he said as they left the kitchen. He switched out the light behind them, and his voice was as abrupt as the cessation of electric current.

Katherine was furious that Jace had initiated the confrontation. Attack was the best strategy, and now he held that advantage. Blast him!

"All right," she snapped. She sat down in the chair opposite the couch. "I want to talk to you too."

Jace settled himself on the edge of the sofa and stared at his hands hanging between his knees. "I should have told you about Lacey. I apologize. I'm sorry you had to find out about her the way you did."

"I'm sure you were," she sneered. "I believe I barged in on a romantic reconciliation."

"Not exactly," he said tersely. His chiseled face which had softened with his apology was now becoming stern. The black wing eyebrows lowered over glowering eyes.

"No? Oh, of course, you have the handicap of a wife now, don't you? How unfortunate. But then I doubt if that small detail will have any bearing on you and Lacey resuming your relationship."

"Dammit," he cursed softly. He was rubbing his knuckles together in extreme agitation. "You're always so automatically goddamned defensive. You just won't try to understand, will you?"

"Understand?" she asked on a high note. "I walk into my husband's office and find him in an embrace with a beautiful, chesty woman who just happens to be his former wife," she paused to draw a deep breath, "and I don't understand?"

"" .lous?" he asked with a glimmer of the humorous mischief that often danced in his eyes.

His shift of moods disconcerted her. *Yes!* she wanted to shout. *Yes. For all the time she had with you. Yes. For all of the times when you made love to her. Yes. For each time you kissed her. Yes, I'm eaten up with jealousy.*

Instead she said off-handedly, "Jealous? No. One must be in love to be jealous." Was that a small flicker of pain that crossed his features? No, it was only a pang of irritation that she wasn't showing more distress. "After all, this was a marriage of convenience," she persisted. "We both know why we got into it."

She looked away from him, not able to meet his discerning eyes. Abruptly, she rose and crossed to her desk. She had to put space between them. *Protect yourself, Katherine*, she warned silently.

"I . . . uh . . . it," she stammered. She cursed her inability to stick to her resolve when he looked at her. Staunchly, she continued, "I was upset because you lied to me about my job."

"You'll do a good job, Katherine, no mat—"

"You're damn right I will!" she exclaimed as she spun around to face him. "I'm more determined than ever to do a terrific job. I'll show you and Mr. Willoughby Newton that he doesn't have to patronize me because I'm one of his main boys' wife."

195

Careful, Katherine, she cautioned. She could feel the tears filling her eyes. "For whatever your reasons, you landed me a peach of a job. I thank you, Mr. Manning. But I'm just another employee now. And from here on, I fly alone. If I make it, great. If I don't, then it will be my own failure. But I want no help from you." She enunciated the last seven words precisely, defiantly.

"You're mistaken if you think I would have it any other way, Katherine," he said quietly.

She was taken aback by his calm acceptance of her tirade. Where was his anger? Why wasn't he fighting back? If anything, he looked . . . what? Sad? She struggled to regain some of her impetus.

"As far as our marriage goes, we each go our own way. Under the circumstances, I think that's fair."

"You do." It wasn't a question. Rather it was a barely audible statement.

"Yes, I do," she said with more conviction than she felt.

She was presenting him an open invitation to be with Lacey as often as he wished. Even as she said the words that gave him his freedom, she asked herself how she could bear it if he left her now.

"For Allison's sake, we can go on imitating a family unit, if . . . if you still want to," she struggled on. Pausing, she allowed him ample opportunity to contradict her, and prayed that he wouldn't. When he didn't speak, she continued, twisting her hands together, "I think you and I should . . . should follow our personal pursuits and do whatever we . . . whatever we want to do."

She was finished. Where was the sense of satisfaction she had expected to feel? There was no triumphant elation filling her veins. Instead, an emptiness, ironically as heavy as a stone, was pressing on her heart. Her rehearsed speech had sounded trite, childish, uninspired, and uncertain.

Jace stood, stretched to his full height, and walked toward her. "I think you are absolutely right, Katherine."

She closed her mind to the agony his words brought her. Her lips pressed together to trap a sob that longed to escape. Even now she hoped he would beg her forgiveness and declare an everlasting love for her. Well, she had delivered an ultimatum, and he had accepted it. But she abhorred his ready acceptance. This was one argument she would gladly have lost.

He continued his slow walk until he stood directly in front of her. She felt cornered, suffocated, overwhelmed. His nearness always started a destructive chain reaction in her body. It had done that since she opened her front door and saw him for the first time.

"I think each of us should follow our personal pursuits and do whatever we want to do. And right now, I want to kiss my wife."

She was in his arms before she had time to realize his intention. His mouth closed over hers. There was no violence in this kiss like the bruising one of this afternoon. The force behind it was just as dominating, but the approach was different.

His mouth moved over hers with supplicant precision until, unwillingly, her lips parted to receive his persuasive tongue. He kissed her deeply, thoroughly, and sensually. He didn't move his hands. He only held her tightly against him, making struggling or resistance of any kind out of the question.

She was breathless when, at last, he lifted his head. He looked into her swimming green eyes and slid his arms forward until the heels of his hands were lightly brushing the sides of her breasts under her arms. "Good night," he whispered.

Then he released her, turned, walked into his bedroom, and shut the door behind him. Katherine was dizzy and swayed slightly, though her feet felt nailed firmly to the floor.

Instinctively, her hands reached out for his support. She hoarsely whispered his name. Those now familiar sensations were prickling her body. *Don't leave me like this*, she cried silently.

Then reason returned. And the reason turned to anger. And the anger boiled.

How dare he! How dare he kiss me like that after spending the day with Lacey.

She marched into Allison's bedroom and slammed the door behind her. The racket woke the baby, and she had to be rocked before she would go back to sleep.

Chapter Eleven

❧ ❧

I think I'll start shopping around for firewood. I've seen several ads in the newspaper. Cooper and I thought we'd buy a cord and divide it. One of these evenings, it'll be cool enough for a fire." Jace munched on an English muffin and sipped scalding black coffee while Katherine fed Allison her morning ration of cereal and strained fruit.

When she didn't respond to his attempted conversation, he persisted. "What do you think?"

His easy chatter annoyed her now as it had done all week. Ever since the day her new, wonderful world caved in and left her desolate, he had behaved as if there were nothing wrong between them.

She wished he would shout, throw something, have a temper outburst, anything but maintain this pleasant congeniality. "Whatever you think," she murmured as she wiped Allison's cereal-smeared mouth with a damp paper towel. A week ago she wouldn't have believed they would still be living together by the time the weather turned cold, and now, he was talking about stocking up on firewood.

He had almost broken her implacability the evening he came home and casually announced that the well they had been drilling had come in.

"Why, Jace, that's wonderful!" she exclaimed before becoming irritated with herself for the genuine joy she felt at his good news.

He looked at her quickly and grinned in sheepish pleasure. "Yeah. Katherine"—he rubbed his hands together excitedly—"I never get used to it, you know? I mean each time we strike oil, even if I'm positive before we drill that it's down there, it's like . . . like—" He broke off as he held his palms up and shrugged helplessly. He laughed boyishly. "Well, it's like nothing else."

She wanted to share his happiness, his enthusiasm. She longed to hold him, congratulate him, but—

He rushed on. "I thought maybe we could go out tonight. Leave Allison with Happy and go out to dinner and—"

"No," she interjected sharply. The temptation to ac-

:ept was strong. "I . . . uh . . . I typed for hours today and I'm tired."

His disappointment was apparent, but he smiled kindly and said, "Okay. Some other time."

"I guess I'd better be going," Jace said now as he stood up and stretched, raising his arms high above his head. "I'm glad I bought that bed when I did. It crowds the room, but it's worth it." His smile was dazzling, devilish. She tried to ignore him.

He leaned down and nuzzled the back of her neck. "All it needs to make it perfect is for you to be with me." His lips nibbled at the sensitive skin on her neck, and Katherine's hand shook as she determinedly shoved another spoonful of peaches into Allison's dodging mouth.

Jace's hand slipped under Katherine's arm and covered a breast, squeezing it gently. His hand scorched her skin through the thin cotton of her T-shirt. She dropped the spoon, stood up, and wheeled around to face him. "Don't do that." She strove to control her quivering voice and said more forcefully, "If you want to . . . to play with someone, go play with Lacey." She was encouraged to see his lips compress in irritation. "Besides, her figure is much more . . . generous . . . than mine," she said scathingly.

The metallic coldness in his eyes left no doubt that she had finally succeeded in sparking his anger. His jaw worked in vexation, and he held his whole body rigid as though trying to keep a rein on murderous impulses.

The victory didn't go to Katherine, however. Insolently, he raked her body with those glinting eyes and drawled, "Yes, it is. Much more generous." Then he turned and left the kitchen. A few moments later Katherine heard the front door slam behind him.

Miserably, she slumped down in the chair and gave vent to her tears. "Oh, Jace," she wept. Unconsciously, she placed her hand over the breast which had so recently thrilled to the warmth of his touch. "I miss you," she moaned before she lay her head on the table and sobbed.

She didn't have the luxury of self-pity for long. Allison had been cross and fretful for the past two days. Her usually hearty appetite had waned. Her nose was stuffy, and, later that same day, she started coughing. As the day wore on, Katherine gave up trying to work. Her increasing anxiety over Allison's health prevented her from thinking clearly or generating one creative idea.

By late afternoon the baby was crying piteously and had developed a fever. Katherine paced the floor with her, trying to comfort her with pats on the back and soothing words. The congestion in her breathing passages became more pronounced, and the cough sounded harsher and deeper.

Unsuccessfully Katherine had tried to call Happy, and continued to notice that her car was still not parked in its usual place. When the telephone rang, she reached for it like a lifeline. Jace was calling to say he might be returning home late, but Katherine was so relieved to hear his voice she forgot her pride and resolve to shut him out and quickly told him about the baby's illness.

"Have you called the doctor?" Jace asked when she finished relating Allison's symptoms.

"Yes. He said to give her liquid fever reducer, watch her closely, and call him if she gets any worse."

"When was that?"

"Early this afternoon."

"Well, I think I'd better call him and have him meet me there. Are you okay?"

"Yes," she said anxiously. "But, Jace, it's just that she was so little when she was born, and her lungs—"

"I know, darling, I know. You sit tight, and I'll be there as soon as possible."

Katherine replaced the telephone receiver and felt a glow of love spread over her heart. Jace was coming to help her. Everything would be all right. Jace would be home soon. She whispered such to the crying, coughing Allison as she continued to pace with the infant or rock her in the wicker chair.

Allison became more agitated with each passing minute. Katherine's anxiety turned into terror when the baby's breathing became labored. She emitted a harsh, grating sound from deep in her throat. Her cough sounded like something out of a nightmare. Katherine was reminded of baying hounds.

She was frantic by the time she heard someone on the stairs and rushed to the door, flinging it open with the baby still clutched in her arms. Jace was running up the steps two at a time with Dr. Peterson, Allison's pediatrician, in tow. Jace halted mid-stride when he saw Katherine's wild eyes, but then leaped up the last few steps into the room.

He looked down at Allison as Katherine blubbered, "She can hardly breathe. Listen to her. She's going to die. I know it. Her lungs—"

The doctor and Jace all but ignored her as they looked at Allison. Dr. Peterson heard the hard, wracking cough and said hurriedly, "Into the bathroom."

Jace shoved Katherine toward the specified room. He seemed to know what to do, for he reached for the hot water tap in the bathtub before Dr. Peterson had time to follow them in and close the door behind him.

"What—" Katherine started, but Dr. Peterson interrupted with, "Do you have any Mentholatum, Vaporub, anything like that?"

Katherine nodded dumbly and pointed toward the medicine chest behind the mirror. The doctor grabbed a jar and started liberally spreading the pungent gel on Allison's throat.

Meanwhile, the bathroom was becoming like a steam room with the hot water tap running full strength in the tub. Jace took a towel off a rack and held it under the faucet in the sink, soaking it in warm water. He rung all excess water out of it and placed it gently over the small chest

"I should have known—" Katherine began apologizing for her own ignorance.

"Not if you've never had a child with croup before." Dr. Peterson interrupted her again. "It's one of the most alarming things to experience. It sounds a lot worse than it is." His voice was reassuring, and Jace placed a supportive arm around Katherine's shoulders. Unmindful of the schism between them, she leaned against his hard strength gratefully as the doctor replaced the warm, moist towel over Allison's chest.

He continued his patient ministrations as the minutes ticked by. The three adults in the cramped space were dripping with perspiration when, finally, Allison coughed long and hard. Katherine reached for her, but Dr. Peterson put out a restraining arm. "This might be it," he said.

A bubble of thick mucus sprouted from the baby's nose at the same time she coughed chokingly and spat out what had given them all such grief.

"There we go," the doctor cried cheerfully. He wiped Allison's nose with a tissue and cleaned out her mouth with a gentle, probing finger.

Almost immediately Allison's breathing returned to normal. She lay back sleepily and closed her eyes. For the first time in hours she wasn't crying.

Jace restored the ravaged bathroom. Katherine hovered over Dr. Peterson as he carried Allison into her room. He laid the baby down gently in her crib and pulled out a stethoscope, placing it on the rising and falling chest.

When he straightened up, he said, "Just as I thought. Her lungs are clear. She's probably had a viral cold for the past several days, and got a little clogged up. The harsh breathing and coughing came from her throat, not her lungs."

"Thank you so much, Dr. Peterson. I was so scared."

"I know you were. Just remember the old bathroom trick if Allison or future children ever get croup." He glanced down at Allison and, deciding to give her some medication, administered it into her mouth with an eyedropper.

"That's a mild decongestant, but even so, it should keep her under for the rest of the night." While he filled out a prescription blank he said, "Have this filled tomorrow. You can give her liquid aspirin if she runs any fever and call me if she's no better in a day or two. Do you have a vaporizer?"

"Yes," Katherine answered, aware that Jace had joined them.

"I'd keep it going in her room for a couple of days. It'll relieve her congestion."

"Thank you, Doctor," Jace said, extending his hand for the doctor to shake. He led the pediatrician to the front door.

Katherine was leaning over the crib, stroking Allison's back when he returned.

"She gave you quite a scare, didn't she?" Jace whispered.

"Oh, God, Jace. I was so frightened," Katherine said tremulously.

"I know. I'm glad I called and was able to be here with you." He placed both hands on her shaking shoulders and massaged them comfortingly.

"Thank you," she said softly. Then remembering how expert he had been during the crisis, she asked, "How did you know what to do?"

He laughed softly then said, "When you're on a drilling site out in the middle of nowhere, you learn to be a lot of things. Sometimes we have to act as nurse for one another. One night a man in my outfit got choked up like that and Billy instructed us on what to do."

"Tell Billy I'm forever in his debt."

"He'll like that," Jace said wryly. "Hey, are you hungry? We skipped supper, you know."

"And lunch," Katherine said. She patted Allison's bottom one last time before turning around. "But I hadn't even thought of it."

"Why don't you lie down for a while and let me run out for some hamburgers."

"I hate for you—"

"No problem." He interrupted her on his way out the front door.

Katherine sank down onto the sofa and rested her head on the back cushions, closing her eyes. What a day. . . .

That was her last conscious thought until she awoke to feather-light kisses on her cheek. She opened her eyes and saw Jace bending solicitously over her.

"Did I go to sleep?" she asked drowsily.

"You could've fooled me. Unless you were checking your eyelids for holes," he smiled. "How would you like a picnic?"

"What?" she asked struggling to sit upright. "Oh, Jace!" she exclaimed when she saw the hamburgers, french fries, and malteds spread out on the candlelit coffee table in front of her.

"Milady's dinner is served," Jace said with a swooping bow.

For the first time in weeks Katherine laughed out loud at his clowning. That set the mood for their cozy dinner. He regaled her with stories of his ventures abroad. His description of a sheikh who had fancied him as a husband for one of his twelve daughters caused tears of mirth to roll down Katherine's face.

"You're laughing, and I barely escaped with my virtue intact," Jace said with feigned indignation.

Katherine stood up and began gathering the paper plates and cups. Her hands came to a complete standstill when Jace grasped her around the waist and turned her to face him as he sat on the sofa.

Exercising no will of her own, she followed his lead and was drawn closer. His hands ran up and down her back as he stared into her eyes.

"No bra today," he whispered roguishly, flashing that mischievous smile she had come to adore.

Holding her eyes with his, he reached under her T-shirt with caressing hands. Her own eyes swam with emotion as she felt his tentative fingers on her flesh. She didn't deter him. She wanted this. She would review her regrets later. For right now she gloried in his touch.

He raised the shirt and slipped it over her head. Honey-colored hair tumbled down around her shoulders. The candles were the only illumination as he viewed her body. The flickering candlelight shaded and highlighted the hollows and planes in a study of sculpture.

Jace buried his face between her breasts and kissed the soft flesh. His words were muffled. "Katherine . . . beautiful . . . sweet . . ."

He kissed her breasts tenderly, almost reverently. He pulled back and worshiped them with his eyes as his fingers paid homage. Then he kissed them again.

Looking at him from this angle, Katherine saw that his black eyelashes were thick and spiky. His nose was perfectly shaped—long and straight and aristocratic.

He clasped her behind the knees and moved his hands up the backs of her thighs. Her heart pounded in anticipation. Spontaneously, she placed both hands on his head and bent hers over it, draping that beloved head with her hair.

His hands circled her waist then moved to her stomach. He unsnapped her jeans and slid the zipper down her abdomen. Slipping both hands into the opening, he settled them on her hips.

"Katherine," he breathed, "your complexion is golden and beautiful all over." He nibbled her stomach. The stubble on his chin abraded her skin, but it was a pleasant sensation.

His hands clenched her tighter as his mouth encompassed her navel. He took it leisurely, nibbling it with his teeth and exploring it with his tongue. He attacked it, made love to it. It was a warm and possessive and totally sexual assault.

Katherine's breath was coming rapidly. Small explosions of sensation erupted from her throbbing femininity and suffused her with fire. She had too much blood for her veins to contain, and it flooded riotously through her body.

Jace pulled back and studied the lacy elastic band on her bikini panties. He hooked his finger under it and traced a mesmerizing line first to one side of her abdomen, then to the other. His finger came back to its starting point just under her navel. With slow precision he began to lower it.

Just when Katherine thought she would cry out with suppressed emotion, Jace withdrew his hand and stood up abruptly, nearly unbalancing her. He cradled her face between his palms and hungrily sought her mouth. "I can't take this anymore," he muttered thickly. He extinguished the candles quickly and propelled her into the bedroom with him.

Tossing back the covers with an impatient carelessness, he eased Katherine onto the bed. She didn't hesitate to remove her jeans and panties while he flung off his clothes, hissing deprecations to contrary buttons, buckles, and snaps.

When they were both naked, he covered her body with his. He rained fervent kisses on her face and threaded his hands through the golden strands of hair fanning the pillow.

Desperately he whispered, "Katherine, don't deny me this. Please. I want you. I need . . . ."

Her body answered for her. It was unreservedly acquiescent to his demands. Her hands smoothed over the broad expanse of his back, down over his hips, and as far as she could reach on his thighs. It was longing frustrated by abstinence that compelled her to meet his passion equally.

They became one without pause. Jace ceased his frantic kisses and lay his dark head beside hers on the pillow, breathing deeply. Katherine rested her hands on the lean muscles of his hips. They were content to savor the sensation, the satisfaction, the bliss of their bodies being joined in this timeless intimacy.

After long moments Jace supported himself on his elbows as he gazed down into her face. "I knew you were ready or I never would have—"

"I know," she whispered back, brushing back the raven waves that lay damply on his forehead.

He traced the features of her face, sliding his finger

across her cheekbones, down her nose to her lips. His lips followed the path.

"Being like this with you . . . it's . . . oh, Katherine, kiss me," he rasped. She could feel that his body was demanding more now that the initial frustration had been appeased.

She drew his tongue into her mouth and then searched the depths of his with her own curious exploration. He drew apart from her slightly and cupped a breast in each hand, pushing them upward to meet his eager lips. His velvet-rough tongue painted each rosy crest with a warm wetness before it was suckled with his mouth.

Katherine cried his name joyously as she lost all consciousness of anything except Jace's body bringing her to fulfillment. No small component of that fulfillment was hearing Jace call her name in his own crescendo of ecstasy.

※ ※

"I want to check on Allison." Katherine said into the darkness a short while later.

"Who?" Jace asked jokingly. He dodged her playful slap and said, "I'll come with you."

They giggled like naughty children as they stumbled naked through the dark house. Jace managed to bump into and fall over everything he possibly could and blindly groped for Katherine for support. Invariably, he grabbed some intimate part of her anatomy, apologizing profusely as he did so.

"Oh, forgive me, milady. I'm so sorry. It's damned dark in here you know."

Katherine giggled. "You don't need a light. You know where everything is."

"You're absolutely right," he said with a lecherous growl and pinched the fleshy part of her bottom.

"Jace! In front of the baby?"

They both laughed at their foolishness, but became serious as they looked down into the crib. Allison was sleeping peacefully. Her even breathing kept cadence with the soft, hissing steam coming from the vaporizer.

"I don't think she even missed us," Jace whispered.

When they were back in the large bed lying on their sides with Katherine's back intimately pressed into Jace's chest, she had the first pangs of regret over what had happened.

Was she being naive and idealistic to think that sex should be an extension of love? She loved Jace, and sex was certainly a part of her love, but she knew that he didn't love her.

Yet, surely, he felt some emotion toward her. He seemed to enjoy being with her. Earlier, he had been as afraid for Allison as she was. Perhaps for him, that affectionate concern was the extent of his loving.

One thing was certain. She wouldn't allow herself to suffer again the way she had the last few weeks. If this was all she could have of him, then this is all she would demand. It would have to be enough.

As if endorsing what she had resolved, Jace stirred in his sleep and moved his hand from her stomach to a breast, cupping it lightly before his fingers once again relaxed.

Katherine wordlessly mouthed something she would never admit in the light of day. "I love you, Jace."

Katherine sat at her typewriter staring off into space. She was supposed to be working on the copy for the first series of commercials, but delicious memories of last night fogged her brain and stimulated her body until coherent thinking was impossible.

Allison was feeling better. She had regained some of her appetite, and the prescription that Dr. Peterson had given her helped clear her head of congestion and made her drowsy. She was peacefully sleeping a healing sleep.

Katherine had set a goal for today and was determined to achieve it before putting aside her work to start dinner preparations. She typed a few more words before the telephone rang.

It was a surprise to hear Billy's gruff voice on the other end of the line.

"Hello, Billy," she said happily. "What can I do for you?"

"Well, Katherine, I hate like hell to have to make this call." Katherine's heart squeezed painfully in her chest. Something had happened to Jace. NO! An accident? Was he hurt?

"Jace?" she asked on a high pitch.

Billy must have gleaned her train of thought, for he hastily assured her, "Jace is all right. I mean he's not hurt or dead or anything."

Katherine's knees buckled and she sank down gratefully in the nearest chair. "You gave me quite a fright, Billy."

"I'm sorry, Katherine." Was that a stream of tobacco juice she heard whizzing past the receiver of the telephone? "You see, Jace asked me to call you, and I hate to have to tell you that he won't be home tonight."

"Is there trouble with the well?"

Another expectoration. "Not exactly," Billy hedged.

"Then what?" Katherine asked, becoming exasperated with this beating around the bush.

"He went to Longview to get that Newton bitch out of trouble." She heard Billy sigh in relief as he finally delivered the message.

"I see," Katherine murmured, not risking to say anything more, for fear of revealing the swelling in her throat.

"The hell you do," Billy countered. "But that's your and Jace's business. Anyway, that slut called up here an hour ago, blubbering and carrying on. Seems she got in some trouble in a cowboy honky-tonk that appeals to lonely, frustrated housewives. She begged Jace to come over there. He did," Billy sounded disgusted.

"Of course," Katherine sighed. "Th-thank you for calling, Billy. I would have been worried when he didn't come home."

"Well, I don't know when to tell you to look for him. That broad . . . I mean . . . she . . ." Billy's voice trailed off and Katherine saved him from further embarrassment.

"Yes, I understand, Billy."

She broke off the connection before he had time to reply. She buried her face in her hands and shook her head, denying that Jace could leave her for Lacey. After last night? Impossible! After this morning, when he was at the drugstore before it opened to pick up Allison's medicine? No!

How could he kiss her with such tenderness and passion only to rush to Lacey's arms a few hours later? Was that to be the pattern of their lives from now on? Was she to share his passion with Lacey, while Lacey had the added benefit of his love?

"I don't know if I can do that," Katherine said aloud, and only then realized that she had made a decision.

Chapter Twelve

❧❧

Hi, honey.'' Katherine sat at her desk frozen in angry surprise as Jace let himself in the front door and then crossed the room to lean down and kiss her on the cheek. "Boy, I'm beat. Is there any coffee left?''

"I think so," she answered stiffly.

She watched his back as he walked into the kitchen chatting as though he had only stepped out for a newspaper—two days ago. He was remarking on the weather, asking after Allison's health, and expressing disappointment when informed she was down for her late morning nap. He didn't mention anything about where he had been for the past two days and what he had been doing with Lacey Newton Manning.

Katherine had lived in a vacuum since getting the telephone call from Billy. Jace had run to Lacey. He had been gone for over two days without one word. Did he expect to come home and resume life where they left off? Was he going to act as if nothing had happened? Well, it wasn't going to be that easy for Mr. Jason Manning.

"How's the work coming?" he asked her as he came back carrying a steaming mug of coffee. He collapsed onto the sofa and lay his head back on the cushions, closing his eyes briefly. He opened them and looked at her with a perplexed expression when the answer to his question was so long in coming. She saw the purple shadows around his eyes and the dark stubble of neglected beard. He looked gaunt under his dark tan.

"It's going well," she replied after a moment. "I got a letter from Mr. Newton yesterday commending me on the first drafts I sent him. I also talked to the production chief at the television station. He's already scouting out locations for videotaping."

"Hey, that's great. I knew you could do it. I'm proud of you."

She stood up from the chair at the typing desk and went to stand in front of the windows. Her back was to him as she said, "I suppose you're relieved too. Now you won't have to feel so responsible for me."

A long moment of silence yawned between them.

When he spoke, his voice had a distinct edge to it. "What's that nebulous remark supposed to mean?"

Katherine swallowed, trying to suppress the anguish which was twisting her heart. She straightened, put on a cold, unemotional face, and forced herself to face him, turning around slowly.

"That means," she said testily, "that I think we should put an end to this travesty we call a marriage." If the words she had spoken didn't kill her, she was sure the heartache would. Determinedly she continued, unable to meet the piercing eyes boring into her from beneath hooded lids.

"Y-you have other . . . interests . . . and I have always been independent. I don't like having someone else managing my life all the time." Why couldn't she keep her tone firm? Her voice was wavering in accordance with her resolve. She hated to admit that his increasing anger and accusing eyes unnerved her.

"I see. You've got it all figured out," he said bitterly.

"Yes," she averred.

"You can't accept Lacey's existence."

She was stunned that he would verbalize the source of their immediate problem, but she didn't hesitate in retaliating. "No, I can't. I can't accept—"

"You can't accept *me*! You haven't accepted one goddamn thing about me since I walked through that door the first time." He stood up and came stalking toward her in angry strides. She took an instinctive step backward.

"You see!" he shouted, indicating her retreat. "That's what I'm talking about." He stopped a few feet from her and demanded, "What got you on my case, anyway? Huh? Why was I automatically the boogeyman in all of this?"

She only stared at him, riveted to the floor in fear of the fierce temper she had seen exhibited before.

"Answer me, dammit!"

"Because you're a Manning," she lashed out. Her heart pounded in her temples and she gulped for breath. Now that the showdown had come, she feared and dreaded it.

"I was hurt by your family once before, and I don't intend to open myself up for any more pain."

"My family. Not me," he asserted.

"Isn't it the same thing?"

"No! Haven't you learned by now that my values are as different from theirs as night is from day? My God!" He slammed one fist into his other palm.

"Not necessarily." Katherine was warming up to her argument now. She was intimidated by the anger which emanated from every pore of his body and flashed like fireworks out of his eyes, but she was determined to state her case and make it sound convincing. She couldn't tell him that it was impossible to live with him when he was in love with another woman. That was an untenable situation when she was in love with him herself.

"You have behaved just as I expected you to, Jace. You're manipulative, charming your victims into letting down their defenses, then moving in for the kill. What small amount of trust I was beginning to have in you, you've betrayed.''

"Oh, shi—'' He bit off the expletive. After raking frustrated fingers through his unruly hair, he put his hands on his hips and surveyed her with undisguised contempt. "You're a sanctimonious, suspicious bitch. Did you know that?''

"There!'' She pointed an accusing finger at him. "You've just proven my point. Peter used abusive language to my sister. Mary admitted to not even understanding all he called her. But that was only the first round. Later he resorted to physical abuse. Allison is the result of rape. Did you know that? Can I look forward to such manhandling from you? You're doing everything else right on schedule—even to seeing your ex-wife-turned-mistress and flaunting her under my nose. Peter taunted Mary with his affairs with other women too.''

He was across the space that separated them in two long strides. He gripped her upper arms with fists that were made of steel and drew her up close against him.

Through gritted teeth he growled, "I warned you never to compare me to Peter, Katherine. He was a monster. Do you understand that? From the time we were children, he was destined to ruin. He murdered my first puppy and left a note on my pillow telling me where I could find it buried. He raped one of the maids' teenage daughters. I think she was about thirteen. She came to our house after school to meet her mother. Of

223

course, it was hushed up. Money changed hands." He gripped her arm harder and asked bitterly, "Am I going too fast for you? I'll give you all the gory details if you wish."

"Jace, please—"

"Oh, no, Miss Katherine. You want to know what we Mannings are all about, and I don't want to disappoint you." He released her arms and turned away abruptly. He stuffed his hands deep into his jeans pockets and paced the floor as he continued.

"Naturally, he was the apple of my parents' eyes. He was the heir apparent; I was superfluous, a fact I was constantly reminded of. As a boy I sometimes wondered why I wasn't showered with such indiscriminate love and devotion. I resented their preference for Peter when I was a kid, but I'm glad about it now. I would have become just like him. You see, they loved him, but they loved in the wrong way. They were too ignorant to see that. It took me years to figure that out. Years of too much booze and rowdy brawls and wasted energies feeding reckless adventures. One day it occurred to me that if I were going to be a decent human being, I'd have to do it on my own. I was determined that they wouldn't ruin my life."

Katherine covered her mouth with a shaking hand to keep from crying out. If she could have taken back some of the hurtful words she had said, she would. But it was impossible.

Jace wasn't speaking to her now. He was analyzing things in his mind as he articulated them.

"I grieved for poor Mary. I know she must have felt like Daniel in the lion's den. I guess it was time for Peter to marry. Good for the banker's image and all that crap. But I couldn't figure out why Peter would marry someone like her, and why my parents would allow such a match. Then it occurred to me. If he had married one of the set, at his first indiscretion, that woman would have run home screaming to Daddy, or worse, the press, and Peter would have been faced with a big scandal. But sweet, naive, little Mary, an orphan with only an older sister to watch out for her wouldn't make such a scene. She would stoically suffer the slings and arrows, so to speak."

He stopped pacing and drew a deep breath. He stared at Katherine for a long time, his eyes straining to focus through his fatigue.

"Jace, I'm—"

He held up both hands, palms out as if warding her off. "Please, Katherine, I don't want to hear anymore. I'm tired." He squeezed his eyes shut and rubbed them hard with his middle finger and thumb. "I think you've said what you had to say, and I've responded. Let's leave it at that."

He leaned down to retrieve the keys to the jeep lying on the coffee table and started toward the door.

"Where are you going?" she asked timidly.

"To work. I was going to take the day off, but under the circumstances . . ." He allowed his voice to trail off as he shrugged.

When he reached the front door he turned around and faced her. "You're right, Katherine. Feeling as you do, I think it would be best for all of us if we called a halt to this . . . 'travesty we call a marriage.' Was that an accurate quote?" Katherine's heart shattered into a million pieces, each shard splintering her soul.

"And if that's the case," he continued in that flat, unemotional voice, "one of us will have to give up Allison."

Katherine put a clenched fist over her aching chest and her mouth formed a small O. "W-what do you mean?" she asked tremulously.

He stared at her from squinting eyes, his mouth a firm, hard line. "You're so smart, you have all the answers, so you figure it out. Just remember how vicious we Mannings can be when anyone stands in our way."

The door slammed behind him.

Katherine moved through the next few hours like an automaton, feeding Allison and attending to her own needs like one drugged. She clasped the baby to her and wept. She didn't fear Jace would carry out his last veiled threat, but she despaired over her thwarted love for him.

It was hopeless. She had wounded him too deeply for

him ever to forgive her the suspicions she had harbored against him. She may have been wrong about his motivations, his values, his character, but one thing she did know—he was proud. That pride would keep him from ever coming back and trying to reestablish the tenuous relationship they had had before.

Pride and Lacey.

Katherine was vaguely aware of the wail of the fire engine sirens but was too absorbed in her own wretchedness to notice how many were screaming through the streets on their way out of Van Buren.

It wasn't until she heard someone thumping up the stairs that she was jarred out of her lethargy. Could it be Jace? Her heart skipped a beat, but then plunged back into gloom. She recognized the heavy footsteps to be Happy's. But the large woman was certainly moving quickly.

Katherine met her at the door.

"Katherine, poor dear. Don't get upset until we know what's happened." Happy's lower lip was quivering. Her laughing eyes were clouded with anxiety.

"What are you talking about?" Katherine asked dazedly, but a premonition of disaster was creeping up her spine and she shivered. Memories of the night Peter and Mary died flashed through her mind like a slide show.

"Dear, didn't you even hear the fire trucks?"

"Yes, but—"

"It's the oil well, Katherine. There was an explosion."

"My God!" Katherine screamed, then hurriedly covered her mouth in an effort to stem the hysterical screams she could feel bubbling into her throat.

"Now, we don't know all the details—"

"Can you keep Allison?" Katherine was already hurrying toward the bedroom to grab her purse and shove her feet into a pair of loafers.

"Katherine, you can't be thinking of going out there! Why it's still dangerous. The radio is begging people to stay away."

"I'm going. Are you going to take care of Allison or will I need to make other arrangements?" Katherine hated to be so horrid to her friend, but she could brook no arguments now. She had to see about Jace. What if—? Oh, God, no! It just couldn't be.

"Katherine, you know I'll stay with the baby. I'll take her to my house and she'll be there in good health when you pick her up, no matter when it is." Happy sounded offended, and Katherine stopped long enough to hug her quickly. Then she abruptly clasped Happy to her, desperate for Happy to imbue her with strength.

"Thank you, Happy, for—Oh, Happy! Jim?" She only now remembered that Happy's son could be in danger too.

"Today's his day off. Thank the Lord. He went to Dallas." She gave Katherine a shove. "Well, if you're going, go. Call me when you find out anything. Nothing has happened to Jace. I just know it." The landlady's eyes were strangely moist.

Tears glittered in Katherine's own eyes as she said, "I hope you're right. I couldn't stand it if—" She didn't even allow herself to vocalize what she was thinking. She ran down the stairs and out to the parked station wagon.

❧ ❧

It became impossible to negotiate the bumpy road and, at the same time, try to tune the car's radio to a station that was giving reports on the fire. Katherine gave up in desperation. Perhaps it was better if she didn't know.

She wept and prayed and cursed herself. Jace had to be alive! Even if he were disfigured or burned or whatever, he must be alive. Such thoughts made her nauseated, and she swallowed the bile that filled her mouth.

She prayed, "God, if he hates me, that's all right. If he wants Allison, I'll give her up. Just don't let him be dead. I love him. If he must die, let me tell him that I love him first. Don't let him be in pain. Burned. Oh, God, I can't bear it."

He hadn't even planned on going to work today. He had said he wanted to stay at home. Her ugly accusations had driven him out of the house. It was her fault he was at the oil well today.

The landscape was blurred and watery through her tears. She followed the column of black smoke that boiled up over the pine forest like Moses followed the pillar of fire in the wilderness. It could be seen for miles. It was surely a grim harbinger preparing her for the devastation she would find when she reached the drilling site. She saw several news helicopters buzzing toward the fire like vultures to a carcass. She resented and cursed them. Night after night, she watched the news reports on television with graphic pictures of train wrecks and car accidents and fires. Did the families of those victims resent such invasions of their privacy? Katherine hadn't realized until now that their suffering was real. Those stories weren't for the television viewer's entertainment. They were personal, human tragedies.

She was surprised to see the top of the derrick. It wasn't the well that had exploded then. There were cars and pick-up trucks and fire-fighting vehicles parked in a semi-circle around the drilling site. She braked the station wagon and jumped to the ground, running pell mell toward the fire which she could now see was isolated to an area near—the trailer!

"Hey, lady!" Strong arms grabbed her around the waist, and she fought like a wildcat to be released. "You can't go over there. You're liable to get hurt." The fireman in the bright yellow slicker cursed expansively when she bit the hand that was restraining her across the chest.

"I think you'll find she's hard to convince." The calm, deep voice penetrated Katherine's frantic mind and she suddenly collapsed in the startled fireman's arms. He would have dropped her if another pair of arms hadn't helped him support her.

"Jace," she whispered disbelievingly as she looked up into his blackened face. "Oh!" she exclaimed, alarmed by his appearance.

"No, I'm not charred, just dirty," he assured her.

"Oh, darling, darling," she buried her face in his shirt and hugged him tight around the waist. "I was so worried. I thought . . ." Emotion clogged her throat and she clutched him even tighter.

"Come over here and I'll explain what happened." Jace extricated himself from her pythonlike embrace. As he steered her away from the scene, she caught sight of the fireman, still nursing his injured hand.

"I'm sorry," she apologized. "I thought my husband was hurt and I was acting crazy. I truly am sorry."

He smiled crookedly and said grudgingly, "That's all right."

Jace led her toward her abandoned car with a firm hand under her elbow. When they reached it, Katherine looked up at him with tearful, green eyes and asked, "What happened?"

Jace wiped his forehead with his shirt sleeve. "It looks a lot worse than it is. All the trucks are here because of the surrounding forests. They're really here for prevention more than anything. But," he added grimly, "we should be thankful we weren't all blown to smithereens."

"The smoke—"

"Yeah, oil makes a helluva smoke. Something near the trailer—an electrical wire, telephone cable—something caused a spark large enough to ignite the butane tanks underneath it. It blew sky high. Several barrels had negligently been put in the wrong place. If I'd been here . . ." He clenched his teeth. "Anyway, they went up when the trailer did."

"Billy!" Katherine exclaimed and clutched Jace's arm.

"Luckily, he and I had just stepped out of the trailer to check on that pick-up he's been working on."

When Katherine shivered, he drew her against him. "I've got a great crew, Katherine," he said proudly. "They all dropped what they were doing and reached for fire extinguishers. Others grabbed shovels and started digging trenches around the fire. They reacted like pros."

"They have an excellent boss," she murmured against his throat.

He pulled away from her slightly and looked deeply into the moisture-laden eyes. "You certainly were in a hurry when you got here. What was the rush?" he teased, though his expression was serious.

"I had to find you," she admitted without qualm. "I had to see you, to tell you. I'm sorry, Jace. For everything. I've been such a fool." The tears ran unchecked now. "When I thought you might be . . . Well, nothing mattered anymore. Nothing. Not even . . . what I mean is . . . I love you, no matter what you—"

He didn't let her finish. He cut off her words by lowering his mouth onto hers. She was oblivious to the dirt and grime that covered every visible part of his flesh. She disregarded the acrid smell of smoke that permeated his clothes and hair. All she cared about was the warmth with which he kissed her.

The kiss lacked some of the sensuous passion of others they had shared, but this wasn't a time for passion. This was the time for commitment, and Jace's mouth, clinging to hers, formed a covenant between them.

"Katherine, Katherine, I love you. How could you ever have doubted that? Doubted me?"

"Just stupid, I guess." She smiled up at him.

He chucked her under the chin and said grimly, "As much as I'd like to continue this conversation, I've got a bitch of a job waiting for me. Go home and don't use all the hot water. I may need a bath when I get home." He grinned. "And don't wait up for me. I may be here quite a while."

"I'll be up," she whispered just before she kissed him and reluctantly climbed back into the car.

"Jace?"

"Hmm?"

"Tell me about Lacey."

Jace opened one eye and cocked it toward Katherine. They were lying on the wide bed. The mid-morning sun was filtering through the shuttered windows onto their nakedness. Jace was stretched out on his back, one knee raised. Katherine was lying on her stomach, supporting herself on her elbows as she leisurely perused her husband.

He had returned home sometime after midnight, exhausted and dirty and hungry. While he showered, she fixed him a tall sandwich which he practically swallowed whole before collapsing onto the bed and falling into a deep slumber.

Katherine had tried to pick up Allison, but Happy insisted that the couple spend the day together uninterrupted. Jace needed his rest after the trauma of the fire and didn't need to be disturbed by any of Allison's fussy spells, infrequent as they were. Katherine was delighted with the prospect of having a day to spend alone with Jace and offered no arguments to Happy's proposal that Allison stay with her.

Jace had awakened only an hour ago and hadn't disappointed her. He reached for her immediately and they had made love with tender passion.

Now he stretched both arms above his head and clasped his hands underneath it. "Lacey. Lacey," he scoffed. "I don't know where to start. She was beautiful, the boss's daughter. She came on to me, an ambitious young man who was feeling his oats, and I married her. She played it just right. There was no hanky-panky allowed during our courtship. Imagine my surprise on our wedding night to discover that others had pioneered the way for me. Maybe that's why I was so surprised to learn that my second wife was a virgin." He reached over and kissed Katherine on the nose. She immediately nuzzled it in the hair on his chest.

"Anyway, Lacey was a spoiled brat, somewhat like Peter, I suppose. She was, and still is, bent on destruction. She had one affair after another. After each one she begged my forgiveness during tearful scenes when she threatened suicide amid self-deprecations. I finally got fed up and told Willoughby that in order for me to continue working for him, I'd have to secure a divorce. He handled it. In all humility, I was too valuable for him to let go. And he knew what Lacey was like. His version of love is an inexhaustible checking account. I think deep down, he feels responsible for what he's created."

"What happened when you went to Longview?"

"Jealous?" he asked.

"Damn right," she answered.

He laughed, but became serious when he resumed. "Well, as you no doubt noticed the day you caught us in the trailer, Lacey refuses to accept the fact that we're not married. It doesn't matter to her except to the extent that I'm no longer her captive. She's got plenty of men to keep her company," he said without rancor. "And the fact of the matter is, she's a lousy lover. Her sensuality is all for show. She's to be pitied."

He shifted his weight. "On with the story," he sighed. "She went to this bar in Longview and got into trouble by trying to pick up someone else's boyfriend. When the other woman won out, she became depressed, checked into a motel, took a bottle of sleeping pills, and called me. My initial reaction was to tell her to go to hell, but I couldn't. I don't know''—he shook his head—''maybe it's my allegiance to Willoughby, but I just couldn't ignore her. It was two days before she was able to leave the hospital. I phoned Willoughby to come pick her up. He's promised to see that she gets help of some kind. Whether he will or not, I don't know. But I made it clear to him and her both, that I've had it. I have another wife now that I love dearly, and I don't intend to jeopardize that relationship under any circumstances.''

''You should have called me, Jace, and explained the situation. I would have understood.''

''I realize that now.'' He chided himself with a short laugh. ''There was so much going on that it honestly never occurred to me. I've lived by and for myself for so long, that I'm not in the habit of reporting my whereabouts. I apologize. Besides,'' he added, ''I hated the thought of dragging you into the quagmire of my former life.''

Katherine hung her head shyly, ''You haven't . . . haven't . . .''

''I haven't slept with her since long before our divorce four years ago.''

''And the question of children?'' she asked.

He laughed harshly. "Never came up. She heard about the details of our marriage from Willoughby and couldn't wait to get her barbs in you."

"Why didn't you explain all of this before? When I first met her?"

"What?" he cried incredulously. "And deny you all that lovely sulking and drawer slamming! Sometimes I think that you actually enjoy all your insecurities. Besides," he added, "I'm too proud to have pleaded innocence when there wasn't even a crime."

"Jace." The word was mumbled as she leaned over him and claimed his lips with her own. Breathless from the kiss, she snuggled over his chest and rested her head under his chin. He stroked her back leisurely.

"What would you say to our buying some property and building a house," he surprised her by asking. She raised her head and looked at him. He went on. "I've spotted a beautiful three-acre lot for sale. It's only a mile from town, but a veritable forest of trees gives it privacy. And I don't think we'll fit into this apartment much longer. The walls are closing in."

"Jace, that sounds wonderful," she said excitedly. "But what about Sunglow? Will you be here that long?"

"We'll be drilling in the area for at least three years. After that"—he shrugged—"we'll just wait and see, okay?"

"Okay," she agreed, smiling. "A house," she sighed. "That'll be such fun to plan."

"Oh, Lord, spare me," Jace implored the ceiling.

Katherine laughed and lay her head back on his chest. "What were your plans when you first started looking for me?" she asked sleepily.

He chuckled and the hairs on his chest tickled her nose. "Well, I set out to find Miss Katherine Adams and spank her little fanny for doing such a dangerous, dumb thing. Of course, that was before I saw what a lovely little fanny it was." He couldn't resist smoothing his hand over the object of his admiration.

"Then I was going to use persuasion, reason, money, or force to get you to release Allison into my care. It wasn't that I was against you, Katherine," he explained. "I was afraid that you'd lose a legal battle with my parents and they'd get guardianship of her. I'm glad they didn't, of course." He paused significantly. "But I'm not sure we shouldn't let them see her." He spoke softly and hesitantly. "I know how you might feel about that, but maybe we should give it some thought. Perhaps I'm feeling magnanimous because of my brush with death yesterday, but they're probably suffering over everything that's happened too. And Allison might resent us years from now if we didn't provide her with an opportunity to form her own opinion of her grandparents . . . and even Peter."

Katherine was still and silent for a long time. Finally she asked quietly, "Can I think about what you've said and discuss it with you later?"

"Certainly. I realize it hurts for you to remember Mary and everything that happened." He kissed her shoulder lightly. "I have a vile temper, I know. But I'm working on it. I swear I'll make you and Allison happy."

When next she spoke the lightheartedness had returned to her voice. "When you did catch up to me, what changed your mind about forcing my hand?"

"I saw something," he answered. The quality of his voice was altered too. It was husky and deep.

Katherine rose up onto her elbows and looked down at him. "What?" she asked curiously.

"Your face," he replied softly.

"Jace," she breathed.

"To say nothing of the rest of you," he continued with the same stirring inflection. His eyes went to her breasts that were pressing against his chest. He let his eyes feast on their loveliness before bending his head to plant hot kisses into the soft curves.

"I loved you from the first, Katherine. I knew after that first kiss beside Allison's crib that I didn't want her without having you too." His lips became more ardent. "Love me. Please."

Katherine hesitated only a moment before raising herself onto his body and allowed him perfect access to relieve her aching nipples with his obliging tongue.

She positioned herself on his body with an accuracy that astonished him even through this pleasure. "Have you been going to X-rated foreign movies?" he rasped.

"No, of course not." She teased the inside of his ear with her tongue.

"Then how did you learn how to make love so expertly?"

"You taught me, Jason Manning," she whispered before blending her mouth with his.

More
Sandra Brown!

Please turn this page
for a
bonus excerpt
from

HIDDEN FIRES

available
wherever books are sold.

The heat from the September sun was like a physical assault to the young woman who stepped down from the train at the Austin depot. Her ivory cheeks were slightly flushed, and a few vagrant tendrils of raven-black hair escaped the chignon under her hat. She fanned a lacy handkerchief in front of her face as she eagerly scanned the crowd for a familiar brown Stetson, and the tall, white-haired man who would be wearing it.

A sizable throng had gathered at the depot for the arrival of the noon train from Fort Worth. Families embraced returning prodigals, while others waved goodbye to passengers boarding the train. Commissions to write soon and be careful were issued in a cacophonous blend of English and Spanish, with the train's hissing white steam and sharp whistle providing the percussion for this discordant orchestra. With amazing alacrity, porters wheeled long, flatbed carts loaded with luggage, managing to skirt old ladies, businessmen, and young children.

Mexican women dressed in bright, full skirts strolled the platform hawking homemade candy, flowers, and Texas souvenirs. *Vaqueros* leaned lazily against the depot wall, toying with lariats, rolling cigarettes, or squinting at the train they were reluctant to board, for they preferred open spaces and the cerulean ceiling of the Texas sky to the narrow confines of a railroad car.

Many of these cowboys noticed the young woman who watched each approaching carriage expectantly. Her gray eyes, which had been so full of excitement only minutes ago, became clouded with anxiety as the crowd began to diminish. The folds of her skirt swished behind her enticingly as she walked the length of the platform and back again. Dainty, high-button shoes tapped on the smooth boards with each step.

One by one, the *vaqueros* sauntered toward the train bound back to Fort Worth. Most cast one last, longing look at the girl who, despite the heat and her obvious agitation, maintained a cool appearance.

With a screech of steel on steel, a geyser of steam, and a long blast of the whistle, the train slowly inched away from the depot, gained momentum, and finally chugged out of sight.

The platform emptied of people. The Mexican vendors covered the wares in their baskets, and the porters parked their carts in the shade of the building.

The girl in the navy-blue serge suit, white shirtwaist, and tan felt hat stood beside her meager luggage looking forlorn and lonely.

Ed Travers bustled out the depot door, sighted the girl and, tugging his vest over his rotund stomach, hurried toward her.

"Miss Holbrook?" he inquired politely. "Miss Lauren Holbrook?"

The dismayed eyes brightened at the sound of her name and she smiled, parting perfectly formed lips to reveal small white teeth. "Yes," she answered breathlessly. "Yes, I'm Lauren Holbrook. Did Ben . . . uh . . . Mr. Lockett send you for me?"

Ed Travers covered his bafflement with a reassuring smile. "No, Miss Holbrook, not exactly. I'm Ed Travers, the depot manager. I'm sorry I kept you waiting, but the telegraph machine—" He broke off, impatient with himself for bungling what was already a delicate situation. "Forgive me for rambling and forcing you to stand in this heat. Come with me and I'll explain everything." He signaled to a lounging porter, who reluctantly came forward to carry Lauren's luggage.

Mr. Travers indicated the end of the platform by tipping his bowler hat. Still Lauren hesitated. "But Mr. Lockett told me—"

"Mr. Lockett did come for you, Miss Holbrook, but he felt ill and asked—"

"Ben is ill?" she asked quickly, paling and clutching the station manager's arm in alarm.

Her reaction stunned Ed Travers. Why did she keep referring to Ben Lockett? What was this girl to that old buzzard? She was beautiful. No question about that. And Ben had always had an eye for the ladies. Everyone in Texas knew what kind of marriage Ben had with Olivia, but even so, this girl was perplexing. Where did she come from? Why had she come to Texas to see Ben Lockett? She could be no more than twenty, and Ben was in his sixties. Maybe she was a relative. She certainly didn't look like a doxy. And why would Ben be setting up a mistress? He had—

"Mr. Travers, please." Lauren was anxiously waiting for an explanation, and the pleasant, kindly man was studying her with an unsettling intensity. Having arrived after an arduous trip from her home in North Carolina only to find that Ben was not here to meet her was disconcerting enough. Of course, he had warned her that if he couldn't leave Coronado, he would send someone else to greet her. "Is Mr. Lockett ill?"

"Ben?" Travers asked distantly. Then, clearing his throat, he said, "No, not Ben. I guess he sent Jared after you, and he's the one who's sick."

He was leading her down the platform with an encouraging hand under her elbow.

"Jared?" she asked.

My God! She didn't even know Jared! But then, it would be distressing to think that this lovely young woman had anything to do with him. It all came back to Ben. What was his game this time? He had a reputation for practical jokes and surprises, usually embarrassing for the recipient. But would Ben's legendary humor extend to victimizing an innocent like Miss Holbrook? In the few moments he had spent with her, Ed Travers had inferred that Lauren Holbrook was trusting and naive to a fault, uncommon as that was in this third year of the twentieth century.

"Jared is Ben's son, Miss Holbrook," he answered patiently. "Didn't Ben ever mention him to you?"

Lauren laughed easily. "Oh, yes. He told me he had a son. I don't recall if he told me his name, though." Her smile faded into an expression of genuine concern. "He's ill?"

"In a manner of speaking," Travers said gruffly, taking her arm more firmly as they descended the steps to the ground below. Lauren saw a long, flatbed wagon parked several yards ahead of them. The green paint on its sideboards was faded and peeling, the wheels mud-splattered. Its two horses were grazing at a tuft of grass under the enormous pecan tree.

Another horse, a palomino of magnificent proportions, was tied to the end of the wagon. Proudly he tossed his blond mane as if protesting the indignity of being hitched to such a lowly vehicle.

"Apparently, Miss Holbrook, Ben sent young Jared for you, and he came from Coronado last night. This morning, when he became incapacitated, he asked me to escort you to his home. I'm afraid the trip won't be very comfortable. I apologize, but this was the best conveyance I could find on short notice."

"I'm sure I'll be fine." She smiled. Ed Travers became dizzy under the radiance of her face and gentle voice. Then he cursed himself for being an old fool and hastened toward the wagon.

The depot manager assisted Laura onto the rickety seat. As the porter dropped her bags unceremoniously onto the rough floor of the wagon bed, she heard a muffled moan.

She gasped in surprise when she saw the long figure sprawled on his back in the wagon. "Mr. Travers!" she exclaimed. "Is he seriously injured?"

"No," he answered. "Only a little indisposed. He'll live, though he may soon wish he were dead." He mumbled the last few words, and his meaning escaped Lauren.

She settled herself as best she could on the uncomfortable seat. The brown leather was cracked. At intervals where it had ripped open, the stuffing poked through in hard lumps. The rusted springs groaned under her slight weight. She kept her gaze focused on the road ahead.

"I must run back inside for a moment, Miss Holbrook, and speak to my assistant. If you'll indulge me, we'll be on our way without further delays." Ed Travers doffed his hat again and turned back toward the depot. The porter shuffled after him.

Lauren sighed. Well, it's not the greeting I expected, but it's novel, she thought. Then she smiled with the sheer joy of being in Texas and almost at the end of her journey. Had it been only three weeks since she last saw Ben? It seemed like eons. So much had happened since he had visited her guardians and issued the impulsive invitation for her to come to Texas.

They had all been in the parlor of the parsonage. Lauren was pouring tea, which was one of her chores when Reverend Abel Prather and his wife, Sybil, entertained. Guests visited often with the middle-aged couple, who had opened their home to Lauren when her clergyman father died eight years ago. She loved the Prathers, though she realized they were unenlightened about anything outside their sphere. Most of their callers were either other ministers or parishioners.

Their guest on that particular day had been unique. Ben Lockett had served in the Confederate Army with the young Chaplain Prather during the last three years of the war. Their philosophies differed greatly, but the two men enjoyed each other's company and found pleasure in taking opposing sides of any debate, whether over the strength of the Union Army or predestination.

After the war, Ben Lockett had left his native Virginia for unknown parts of Texas. He was of a breed of ambitious, angry young men who defiantly carved empires out of the vast plains of Texas. In the forty years since the War Between the States, Ben Lockett had become an influential cattle baron.

Lauren was intrigued by the imposing Texan. He stood tall and lean, with only the slightest paunch to indicate his advancing years. His hair was thick and snowy white, brushed back from his wide, deep forehead like a crest. Blue eyes twinkled merrily from under shaggy white eyebrows, as if he were perpetually amused by the world. But Lauren observed that

Ben was capable of a piercing, glacial stare if his emotions dictated it.

His voice was deep and mellow when he said to her, "Tell me, Miss Holbrook, what you think of Texas. Like most Texans, I feel that everyone should be as enthralled with my country as I am." He stared at her from under the shaggy brows, but it was a friendly look.

"I . . . I don't know that much about it, Mr. Lockett," she replied honestly. "I've read about the Alamo, and I know that the state was once a republic. The rest of my knowledge is confined to the penny-novel book covers that I see on display at the general store. They depict train robberies, cattle rustling, and saloons. I don't know if that is a true characterization or not."

Ben threw back his head with its shock of white hair and roared with laughter. The booming sound rattled the china figurines that cluttered every conceivable space in Sybil Prather's overdecorated parlor.

"Well, we have our share of train robberies, and I've frequented a few saloons myself, begging your pardon, Abel. I've even chased a few rustlers all the way to Mexico." He paused. "Maybe the pictures you've seen are accurate at that, Miss Holbrook." He studied her for a moment longer, then challenged, "Why don't you come back to Texas with me and see it for yourself?"

There were several startled exclamations.

"Ben, you're joking, of course! I'd forgotten what a tease you are." Abel laughed.

"Let my Lauren go to Texas where Indians live!"

Sybil cried. The ruffles covering her ample bosom quivered with distress.

"What an utterly preposterous suggestion!" came from William.

William. Yes, William Keller had been there, too.

Lauren shuddered, even in the stifling heat. She pushed the thought of William out of her mind. She wasn't going to let the memory of him ruin her reunion with Ben Lockett.

Another groan, accompanied this time by a mumbled curse, diverted her from her reverie. Hesitantly she swiveled her head to look at the ailing man. Her eyes lighted first on an ornately tooled saddle, with filigreed silver decorations glittering against the black leather. Her bags were at the back of the wagon, near the man's feet.

He must be very tall, Lauren thought as she quickly scanned the length of the prone body. Her initial impression was that he was lean and well proportioned. After that first hasty appraisal, she began at his boots and studied the figure with increasing fascination.

The black boots were of smooth leather and came to just under his knees. Tight black chinos were tucked into the tops of them. Lauren blushed at the perfect fit of the pants, which contoured the long, muscled thighs like a second skin.

Lauren's breath caught in her throat, and she stared as one hypnotized at the bulge between his thighs. The tight pants emphasized and detailed his anatomy. To Lauren, who was raised in deliberate ignorance of the opposite sex, it was a bold display. How could anyone be so flagrantly nonchalant about his . . . person? she wondered.

Her palms grew moist within her gloves.

She forced her eyes to move from his crotch. The buff-colored shirt was shoved sloppily into his belted waistband. Only the last two buttons of the shirt were closed, and the soft fabric fell away from a broad chest that rose and fell with his even breathing. The wide chest tapered to a flat belly and was covered with light brown hair that glinted with golden highlights as the sun filtered through the branches of the pecan tree and shone on him.

Lauren had never seen a man shirtless before. Once a member of Reverend Prather's congregation had caught a deadly fever and she had glimpsed his upper torso as one of the married women in attendance had bathed him. The sufferer was fat; his skin was pink; and his chest was smooth and hairless. No, he had looked nothing like this.

Lauren swallowed hard and pressed her hand against the fluttering in her stomach.

Jared Lockett groaned again, and she held her breath, afraid that he would awaken and find her looking at him with this shameful temerity. But he only sighed, making a deep hollow of his stomach under his rib cage. His hand moved onto his chest, where it stirred restlessly before remaining still. The hand was tanned and large, with strong, slim fingers. The same sun-bleached hair that covered his chest sprinkled the back of his hand.

A strong column of throat extended from the powerful shoulders. Lauren raised her eyes to his face and was crushingly disappointed. His features were covered by a black, flat-crowned, wide-brimmed hat. Her curiosity was piqued by this son of Ben's, and she wanted to view the face that belonged to this long, hard body.

Lauren almost jumped when Ed Travers said briskly, "There. I think we can leave now."

So engrossed was she with Jared Lockett's form that she hadn't noticed the man returning from his errand.

"You are extremely kind to do this, Mr. Travers." Lauren's level voice surprised her. The tickling sensation in her stomach had spread into her chest and throat. These symptoms of "the vapors" were uncharacteristic of the usually serene Lauren Holbrook.

"No problem at all," Travers hastened to assure her.

He clucked to the bedraggled horses and began maneuvering them through the traffic on the streets of the state's capital. They dodged trolleys, buggies, and horseback riders as they made their way through the city. There were no motorcars, which Lauren had seen on recent rips to Raleigh.

She enjoyed looking at the capitol building from the different angles their route afforded her. "I think you're justifiably proud of your capitol building. I've read about it. It's very impressive."

Travers smiled. "The red granite came from a quarry near the Lockett ranch."

"Keypoint," Lauren said. She remembered Ben's proud voice as he told her about the ranch. Her comment on its clever name, which used a play on words with *Lock*ett and *Key*point, caused him to beam at her astuteness. "You'd be surprised at how few people catch that," he said. As he grinned broadly, the furrows on either side of his mouth deepened into facsimiles of dimples.

Lauren smiled at the memory, and Travers glanced at her out of the corner of his eye. So she knew about Keypoint. Did she also know who lived there? Conversationally he asked, "Have you ever been to Texas before, Miss Holbrook?"

"No, I haven't. That's why I was delighted to accept Ben's invitation to come and stay with his family for a while."

The wagon lurched when Travers suddenly jerked on the reins. She was going to stay with them?! In the house in Coronado? Or at Keypoint? Either place was inconceivable. This girl was as innocent as the day was long. Had Ben Lockett gone mad?

They were outside the city now and heading west on the well-traveled road. When Lauren pulled the long pins out of her hat, Travers warned her, "I wouldn't take that off if I were you, Miss Holbrook. Our sun is hot. You might get a burn on that pretty nose."

Lauren agreed and readjusted her hat, but slipped out of her jacket. The slight breeze stirred by the movement of the wagon cooled her damp skin somewhat.

When she was settled again, Travers returned to his thoughts. That wild buck in the back of the wagon was enough reason not to keep any decent woman under the same roof with him.

Jared Lockett was notorious throughout the state for whoring and drinking. When he was younger, his activities had been deemed "sowing wild oats," but since he had passed his thirtieth birthday, they had become a matter of public scorn. When was Jared going to start acting responsibly? No time soon, Travers mused glumly.

Just last month, Jared had caused a big disturbance at the Rosenburg depot. He and some of his feckless cronies had gone into the Harvey House there and had spent the afternoon drinking and gambling. They had made their presence known in the restaurant by behaving like a pack of wild dogs. Jared made an unseemly proposition to one of the more winsome Harvey girls. The girls who worked as waitresses in the restaurant chain that served the Santa Fe Railroad were known for their scrupulous morals. If a man proposed anything to one of those young ladies, it had better be nothing less than marriage and a vine-covered cottage.

When the girl summarily rejected his suggestion, Jared had become more aggressive. The management had ejected him from the place, but not before Jared, fighting like a demon out of hell, had wreaked havoc on furniture, dishes, and a few of the patrons. It had taken six men to subdue him.

Well, sighed Travers mentally, it was probably just as well that this young woman didn't know about Jared Lockett's antics. They would no doubt scare her to death.

"Is it always this hot in September?" Lauren asked,

trying to draw the station manager into conversation. She had had years of practice making small talk in the Prathers' parlor. Mr. Travers had been kind to her, but she was made uneasy by the wrinkled brow and the puzzled expression that would cross his face whenever he looked at her. Was she that different from the women in Texas?

"Yeah," he answered, reassuring her with his easy, open smile. "We usually get our first Norther about the end of October. Most years, September is hotter than June or even July. Is it this warm in . . . ?" He let the question trail off suggestively, and she didn't disappoint him.

"North Carolina. I lived—live—in Clayton. It's a small town not too far from Raleigh. And no, it's not this hot there in September."

"Is that where you met Ben?" he asked curiously. At her affirmative nod, he prodded, "And what was Ben doing in Clayton, North Carolina?"

Lauren explained the friendship between her guardian and the rancher. "For years, they corresponded, but the letters had lagged for the past decade or so. Still, on his way home from a business trip to New York, Ben decided to pay his old friend a visit."

"How long have you lived with this guardian?" Was he being too nosy? He didn't want to offend her, and no man in his right mind would cross Ben Lockett. However, she answered him readily enough and without self-consciousness.

"My father was a clergyman, too. Abel Prather was

his bishop. I was twelve when my father died. The Prathers gave me a home with them."

"Your mother?" Travers asked quietly.

"I was three when she died giving birth. The baby—a boy—was stillborn." Her voice was suddenly soft and pensive. Travers noted that she touched the brooch watch pinned to her shirtwaist just above the gentle swell of her breast.

The small brooch was all she had of her mother's possessions. That and a picture taken of her parents on their wedding day. She vainly tried to remember moments she had shared with the pretty, petite woman in the picture, but no memories would come. Lauren had no inkling of the personality that had lived behind the shy eyes captured in the photograph. In stressful times, or when she longed for the parent she couldn't remember, she touched the watch with her fingertips as if the action brought her in contact with her mother. But this was a habit Lauren wasn't conscious of.

After his young wife's death, Gerald Holbrook had totally dedicated himself to his work. He delved into religious dogma and contemplated theological doctrines in the hours when he wasn't actively serving his congregation or preparing his inspired sermons. If the care of his young daughter fell to his current housekeeper, that was the price one had to pay for absolute commitment to Christ. Lauren knew that, in his way, her father loved her and wasn't bitter over his neglect—though she felt it. She would have welcomed a more demonstrative relationship, but knew her father lived on a higher plane—like God.

She was a well-behaved child, quiet and unobtrusive as she sat near her father when he studied in his library. She learned to read at an early age, and books and the characters in them became her playmates and confidantes. Her classmates weren't particularly inclined to include the "preacher's kid" in their pranks. Out of loneliness, Lauren acquired a talent for creating her own diversions.

When Gerald Holbrook died, Lauren barely missed him. She moved into the Prathers' house and assumed their routine without question. They were kind and, because of their childlessness, welcomed the adolescent girl into their home. Their generosity extended to giving Lauren piano lessons. She was musically gifted, and the piano became a passion along with literature.

No one ever left the Prathers' gaudy, crowded house without knowing their pride in Lauren. She had never betrayed their trust or disappointed them.

Except with William. How unfair was their changed attitude toward her! She was blameless!

"Miss Holbrook?" Ed Travers asked for the third time, and finally succeeded in gaining her attention.

"I'm sorry, Mr. Travers. What did you say?" Lauren flushed under her hat at being caught so deep in her own thoughts.

"I asked if you would like a drink of water," he said, reaching under the seat for a canteen, which he had filled before leaving the depot.

"Oh, yes, thank you." Lauren reached for the canteen. Never having drunk from one, she felt like a pioneer as she tipped it back and took a tentative, ladylike sip.

Just then, the wagon hit a deep rut in the road, and some of the water sloshed onto her shirtwaist. She wiped her dripping chin and laughed delightedly. Her merriment was checked when the figure in the back of the wagon groaned and cursed vehemently.

"Sonofabitch!

To read more, look for *Hidden Fires*
by Sandra Brown.

SANDRA BROWN is the author of over sixty books, of which over fifty were *New York Times* bestsellers, including the #1 *New York Times* bestseller *The Alibi, The Crush, Envy, The Switch, Standoff, Unspeakable, Fat Tuesday, Exclusive, The Witness, Charade, Where There's Smoke,* and *French Silk.* Her novels have been published in more than thirty languages. She and her husband live in Texas.